P9-AOS-314

PRAISE FOR
ERIC LAROCCA

"There's something wrong with Eric LaRocca, and I mean that in the very best way possible. His stories stick a screw right into your heart-meat. Looking forward to whatever gut-clenching horror he has coming."
~ Chuck Wendig, New York Times bestselling author of *The Book of Accidents*

"LaRocca proves that the sickest minds can have the biggest hearts – he's a twisted, tender new talent."
~ Daniel Kraus, New York Times bestselling author of *The Living Dead*

"With darkly poetic prose and chilling stories that peel back layers of skin to reveal a beating, bloody heart, Eric LaRocca is the clear literary heir of Clive Barker."
~ Tyler Jones, author of *Criterium* and *The Dark Side of the Room*

"Eric LaRocca is a fierce talent that knows no limit, masterful and utterly unmissable!"

~ Ross Jeffery, Bram Stoker Award nominated author of *Juniper* and *Tome*

"Eric LaRocca is truly original, truly subversive, and truly talented."
~ Priya Sharma, author of *Ormeshadow*

"With an Eric LaRocca story, you never know what you're getting into. And I say that with admiration... Blazing creativity meets ferocious writing."
~ Jonathan Janz, author of *The Raven* and *The Siren and the Specter*

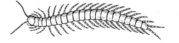

You've Lost A Lot Of Blood

Copyright © Eric LaRocca 2022

Eric LaRocca has asserted his right under the Copyright, Designs and Patents Act 1988 to be identified as the author of this work.

This book is a work of fiction and, except in the case of historical fact, any resemblance to actual persons, living or dead, is purely coincidental.

Independently Published

Paperback 1st Edition 2022

eBook ISBN: 978-1-0880-1420-2

Paperback ISBN: 978-1-0880-2575-8

This book is sold subject to the condition that it shall not, by way of trade or otherwise, be lent, resold, hired out, or otherwise circulated electronically or made free to view online without the publisher's prior consent in any form of binding cover other than that in which it is published, and without a similar condition, including this condition, being imposed on the subsequent purchaser.

Formatting, Editing and Proofreading by Ross Jeffery

Cover Artwork by Kim Jakobsson (kimjakobssonart.com)

Cover Design and Title Page Artwork by Scott Cole (13visions.com)

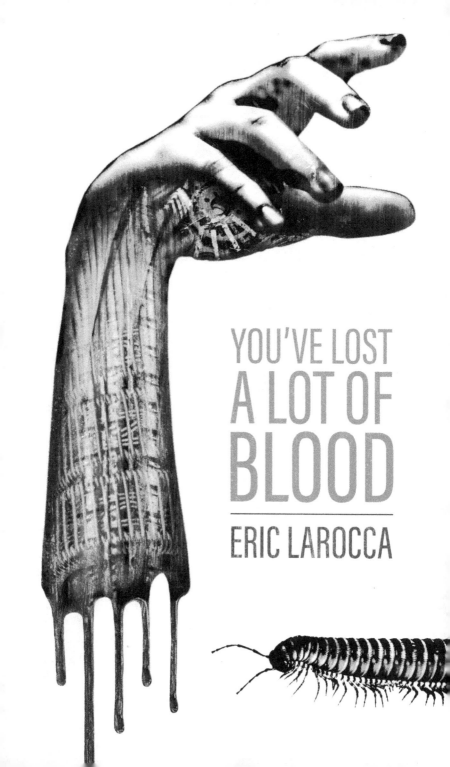

YOU'VE LOST
A LOT OF
BLOOD

ERIC LAROCCA

For those who are lost

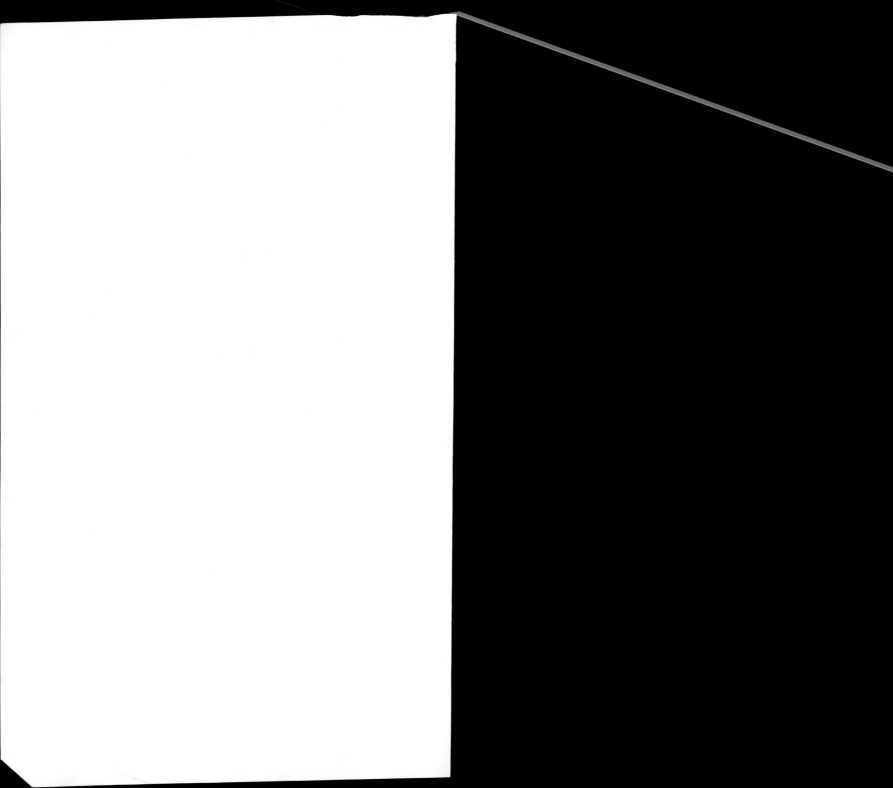

[A NOTE FROM THE EDITOR]

Though much can be speculated when considering the disappearances of Martyr Black and his partner, Ambrose Thorne, there have been great efforts made by all involved in this book who had known them in their lives to preserve the integrity of the writings and documents associated with them.

While there have been countless rumors and falsified reports concerning the reason behind their disappearances, most of these speculations are merely thoughtless fodder for the online communities with which Martyr often engaged before his eventual vanishing.

I knew both Martyr and Ambrose for many years and have needed to come to terms with my own involvement in their unsavory dealings in Schenectady, NY and eventually Chelsea, MA. As I have stated to the police on several occasions during many interviews, I was not present for any of the killings nor was I acquainted with any of the victims.

I first met Ambrose in college when we became lovers—a tempestuous romance soon tempering to more whimsical and delicate fancies as our love became far more cordial and friendly. Not long after graduation, Ambrose became involved with a young man I would come to know as Martyr Black. Apparently raised by a family of noble pedigree, Martyr was everything I anticipated Ambrose might look for in a companion—a charming sophisticate with a penchant for the macabre, for things that were rare, difficult to locate, a gentleman of many experiences and many interests.

From the research I've conducted on Martyr in order to properly compile the information for this manuscript, I've learned that Martyr was originally born in a small town in Georgia but was displaced at the age of three by his parents to the town of Kingston, located in upstate New York. Martyr was a mediocre student at best, his sexual preferences leaning to the bizarre and the outlandish for such an inquisitive and obviously perceptive young man. Teachers were apparently often cross with him for not properly following directions or causing outbursts in the middle of class.

The little information available regarding Ambrose's upbringing confirms him to be an exemplary student, easy to please, and eager to learn. He was born in Vermont and not long after his birth, his father abandoned him and his mother. Struggling to make ends meet, his mother returned to her hometown in Massachusetts and found work at her mother's place of business—a shoe store in Stockbridge.

Neither of these seemingly prosaic upbringings could have informed or precluded the life that Martyr and Ambrose would enjoy together—the horrible things they would do not only to one another, but to others as well.

In the following pages, you will find text written by Martyr Black and dated appropriately. You will also find several poems he had written and published, as well as transcript evidence he had recorded. You will also find the entire text of a novella (titled You've Lost a Lot of Blood) that Martyr Black had published through an independent press specializing in the macabre and uncanny. I've carefully constructed a narrative not necessarily detailing the chronological arc of their crimes and their life together, but rather a narrative to serve an understanding of them as human beings—not as monsters.

While most are rightfully repulsed by the violent nature of their work together, this sensibly curated manuscript is not meant to serve as an insult to the families of the victims. Rather, it's my sincerest hope that these artifacts from an aberrant mind can help better understand his motivations for what he had done *and make it so that no one else suffers again as his victims had suffered.*

Trent Pilcher
Cambridge, MA
April 2021

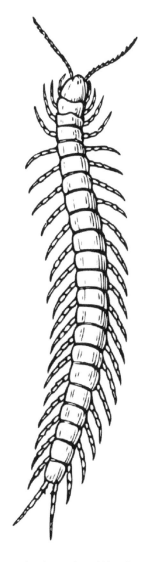

You've lost a lot of blood . . .

RELICS FROM THE NIGHT WE BOTH PERISHED: May 17th, 2019

Each precious thing I've ever shown him is a holy relic from the night we both perished—the night when I combed him from my hair and watered the moon with his blood. An ivory fang stapled against a black curtain like the X-Ray of child's broken bone—a glorious thing to be worshiped, or to at least be acknowledged as "vessel of sorrow," "creator of tides," "pitcher of divine light." He was nothing more than milkweed to be plucked, a discarded plant to be uprooted and torn by the stem until it lies there quivering in your hand—shaking, trembling, frightened.

I didn't kill him because I wanted to.

That would have been too easy.

Far too plainspoken for my preference.

It's the same reason I didn't kill him while he slept in the passenger seat on one of our moonlit drives through the countryside—a container of bleach in my hand and my thumb gently unscrewing the cap. I can so distinctly recall how his ear resembled the perfect drain—a small, shapely spiral circling further and further inside him, carrying obscenities to their resting places tucked away deep inside his darkest recesses. If he had darkest recesses, that is. I knew for certain he was far more benign in his practices, his handling of life and other people.

I killed him because to let him live, to let him exist would have been an insult. It's not that I didn't love him. I certainly would never want you thinking that. Of course, there's a part of me that resents him. Especially late at night when I see his ghost—the ball gag fixed between his chapped lips. He comes to me in dreams—nightmares would imply I detest the thought of them, and I don't, or at least I haven't—and he's dressed in a black satin corset, the breasts I've wished for him hanging out and nipples stiffening like metal screws. There's a giant hole where his face once was, a soundless vacuum sucking him deeper and deeper into oblivion until he's a stain I can smear upon the world—a skull where his thighs come together, a small centipede coiling inside the vacancy of his face. He asks to speak but I tighten the reins securing him as if he were a disgraced show horse—as if he were a black beetle, his wings forever torn off.

I didn't kill him because I found his conversation trite or his knowledge of musical theatre to be abysmal at best. After all, how can I expect any man under the age of thirty to know by heart the entire score to *Chess*[1] by Tim Rice, Benny Andersson and Bjorn Ulvaeus. Of course, the show had its string of hit songs in the eighties, but he was born in the late nineties, and he always referred to me as an "old soul"—a priceless vessel to warehouse the marvelous and the celestial. Yes, he often referred to me as "precious," as if I was marked "Fragile, handle with care." You'd think a young man qualified for even the most menial office job would understand I was the furthest thing from a delicate heirloom—that I was a vile thing, obscene, and unspeakable.

Of course, there's a part of me that still wonders if he knew, if he had somehow known when I came to him and snuffed out the candle I had lovingly tended to and kept burning within him for so long. It was only natural for the wax to melt, for the wick to shorten to a small nub, and for the flame to eventually go out.

I had thought of ending things for a while.

I suppose we all do in some way even if we're content,

dangerously happy with the body we're sleeping next to, with the body we use for sex, for companionship, for love. Little insects—barbed and dangerous with their glittering exoskeletons and their sharp pincers—circle inside my head and whisper indecencies to me. For once, I'd like to see myself outside of myself. If that even makes sense. I'd like to crawl outside of my head and look back at the horrible thing I've become, the soulless spirit residing inside my shell.

For some reason lately I've been thinking of chess. Not necessarily the musical, but rather the actual game. I had always told him that lovemaking, the art of wooing and capitulating to another person was a lot like chess. I don't necessarily know how to play, but I often found the history of chess fascinating. I told him about an automated chess playing machine, known as the Mechanical Turk, invented in the late 17th century—how this automaton toured the most expensive, the most distinguished, the most noble salons in Europe and could never be bested no matter the experience of the opposing player. Being in love with him was very much like executing a game with a mechanical chess-playing machine, I imagine. I knew in my heart that I would always win, that I would never compromise, that I would never let him deep enough inside me to latch on and secure himself as if it were a new home. I knew I never wanted to be his home. No matter how much he begged, no matter how much he pleaded—I'd sooner swallow wet concrete than let him call me his or dare to call him mine.

More importantly, like the Mechanical Turk, our love was an illusion—something that had been invented by others.

I killed him because if I didn't, something might have

tethered us together and that would have been a suffering far too unimaginable for me to even consider. There was something—unnatural—about even the mere thought of us together, let alone the sight of it. I don't necessarily say that because we were two men. I don't want you thinking I'm of the self-loathing variety because:

a.) That's a tired cliché

b.) That's not true

I simply say that because there are moments shared between two people when you realize you're in the room with the wrong person, you're sharing a toothbrush with the wrong mouth, you're sharing a pair of loafers with the wrong feet. There was something distinctly peculiar about the two of us together and I had known it from the moment I had first met him, when he had begged for my attention at the small café where I ordered my coffee every morning. There comes a point when you need to recognize the expiration date of a relationship. For me and him, that date had passed a long time ago and my mind continued to tell me. Of course, at first, I played it off.

"You don't know what you're talking about."

"He's so lovely to me."

"He really cares about me."

The carnage of my thoughts. The privacy I had been afforded. I had killed him many times there—imagined what it might feel like, how he might panic, how he might plead and beg with me. I haven't thought of him much since it first happened—since the night when I first pulled his teeth, plucked his fingernails, and organized them accordingly; as if they were broken remnants, artifacts in the museum of our love: a gallery of yellowing antiquity.

There was a time when I would touch myself, imagining his helpless body fruiting with more decay. In my thoughts,

I would tell him: "you'll find me tucked away in the blistered sinew of what was once healthy and pink, now tender and black." There were many things I imagined doing to him: cracking him open as if he were some expensive delicacy imported from a faraway land and gorging on his entrails until my stomach was fit to burst.

Then, there was the period of time I referred to him as "The Wax Priest"—as if he were a Holy man to be worshiped, to be revered and adored for his anguish. He didn't care much for the nickname and he, of course, never knew the real reason why I referred to him as something so esoteric. The truth is it would have been far more preferable for him to find a lump growing on his scrotum one morning than the plans I had designed for him. It would have been in his best interest to wilt and decay the way an animal carcass does when abandoned in the woods. I yearned for him to flower with cancer—a small ball made of beeswax claiming him and taking him from me.

Unfortunately, that misfortune never came to him.

You're probably wondering how I did it—how I managed to kill the man I supposedly loved, the one I worshiped, adored, fellated even when I was feeling particularly uninspired to perform. I would have never poured bleach in his ears. That would have been far too cruel for a man that deserved a painless ending. I certainly would have never pinned his ears with clothespins and hung him on a rack the way I had seen someone torture a small puppy online when I was nine years old.

Our dance together came to an end not long after his twenty-sixth birthday. There were, of course, things I wanted to say, words I wanted to share before the event— before I squeezed the life from him as if he were nothing more than a child's red balloon, a toy to be discarded after a birthday party. Something that might float up and away on an invisible string pulled by an ancient deity until I'm left standing alone on the chessboard of the mess we've made together—the illusion we had shared, the magic we had wrongfully invented.

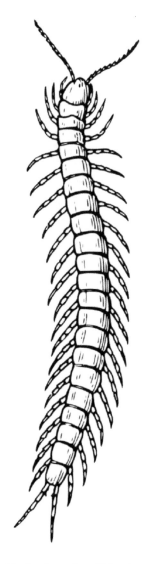

You've lost a lot of blood . . .

YOU'VE LOST A LOT OF BLOOD:
PART ONE

[The following text includes the first three chapters of a novella, You've Lost a Lot of Blood, *that Martyr Black had published by Carter Hill Press in October of 2018.]*

TAMSEN

CHAPTER
ONE

Tamsen, her face twisted in horror, releases a scream so agonizing that it surprises her. A young woman in agony. Filling every inch of the idling car.

She lunges forward in the driver's seat, white knuckling the steering wheel. Screeches until hoarse, her eyes wet and shining.

Just then, her eyes snap to the rearview mirror. She sees her reflection—drenched in black oil as dark as blood. Head to toe.

She glances in the passenger seat: empty cans of motor oil and gasoline. Beside them, a small lighter.

She can scarcely believe it. What had she intended to do?

She straightens, remembering. Panic returns.

"Presley," she says.

Her head jerks to the backseat. There, she finds her brother—a cherub-faced eleven-year-old boy.

He glistens, drenched with oil and stares at her with panic.

Tamsen chokes on quiet sobs, trembling. Eyes dimmed and glassy—forever lost in the nightmare.

—

As Tamsen's car idles in the breakdown lane of the abandoned roadway, she wipes her face with a rag and circles the vehicle.

She pops open the trunk.

In there, she finds the splintered remains of a wooden pine tree carving. Face scrunching, confused, she tosses it aside.

Finally, she uncovers what she's been looking for—two suitcases. She unzips one of them and then grimaces, greeted by a sparkling gold lamé tuxedo suit. Tosses it aside. Reveals a pirate costume.

She spies Presley through the backseat window.

Shoulders slumped, he cleans his face with a rag. His eyes dart to her, concerned.

She waves both costumes at him in the air.

"Pick one," she says.

—

After driving a few miles further up the road, they come upon a small park and a public restroom. Tamsen parks in one of the empty spaces, passes the gold lamé suit to her brother, and then sends him into the men's restroom to wash himself.

Once she's cleaned herself as well, Tamsen meets her reflection in the grime-covered bathroom mirror. She scans her body—from her auburn pixie haircut to the tattoo of two black ribbons wrapped around her ankle.

She twists the rust-eaten faucet. Brown water sputters. She lurches back, disgusted.

Grabs a bottle of hand sanitizer from her bag. Douses her hands with it. A nervous habit.

She winces. The screech of metal against metal pulsing through her head. She doubles over and vomits.

When she's finished dressing in clean clothes, she returns to the car parked out front and starts scrubbing the leather seats clean.

After she's finished cleaning the seats, she rinses the black juices from her washcloth and tosses it aside.

She leans against the car, whips out her phone, and begins to scroll through her missed messages.

Tapping on the screen, she holds the phone to her ear.

The brittle-thin shriek of the woman's voice greets her on the other end. She flinches at the sound.

"Miss Deerling, we're delighted to welcome you as our new lead game developer at the Zimpago Project," the voice tells her. *"All of the information you'll need can be found in the letter we've addressed to you."*

Phone pressed against her ear, Tamsen leans over the passenger seat and digs through the papers scattered on the floor. She recovers a crumpled sheet of paper and unfolds it.

The paper's header—emblazoned with an ornate insignia. "The Zimpago Project." An address: "164 Carter Road. Whitefield, New Hampshire 03598."

"We ask that you have your samples prepared when you arrive," the voice says. *"All lodgings and provisions will be taken care of while you stay with us. We are very much looking forward to working with you."*

The recording ends.

Tamsen taps the screen, reviewing the call log. All her messages—deleted. Except for one. "Unknown Caller."

The screen flickers out, her phone dying.

"Shit."

Tamsen hops in the driver's seat, shoving the keys into the ignition. She grabs the stick shift.

Then, her eyes snap outside the windshield, noticing Presley as he approaches the car.

He's dressed in his sparkling gold lamé Elvis-inspired suit and has a polaroid camera looped around his neck. He slows as he approaches the vehicle, eyebrows furrowing.

Tamsen climbs out of the car. Swallows, uncomfortable.

"Elvis," she says. "Good choice."

"Dad's favorite."

Tamsen pouts at the reminder. She bites her lip, nodding.

Suddenly, she notices her brother's eyes fixed on the vehicle's front grill. She circles the hood, puzzled.

"What is it–?" she asks him.

Presley merely points. Her eyes follow. She sees it –

Her front right headlight: completely shattered. The glittering pieces—broken and hanging like the bits of a cracked eggshell.

"Shit."

Presley corrects her: "Excrement."

Tamsen kneels, inspecting the damage. Presley snaps a picture. The camera whirs alive, printing.

"Did we hit something?" he asks.

"I'll get a ticket if we don't stop to change it," Tamsen says, shoving her hands into her pockets. "I have to ask for directions too."

She huffs, heading back for the driver's seat. Glances back. Notices Presley's still standing there.

"Let's go?"

But he seems to hesitate, as if distrustful.

"What?" she asks. "Did you think I was going to leave you?"

Presley squints, guarding his eyes from the morning sunlight.

"Come on," Tamsen says, flashing him a smile. "Maybe they sell books at the auto part store."

Presley softens.

Tamsen climbs in the car. Presley follows, jumping in the backseat. The car creeps out of the parking lot, easing back onto the road.

CHAPTER
TWO

It's not long before they come upon a small shack fronted with a rickety looking wrap-around porch. Two antique gas pumps are arranged in the parking lot.

Tamsen's car meanders off the narrow roadway, parking beside one of the pumps.

A grizzled gas attendant dressed in flannel and a moth-eaten baseball cap abandons his newspaper and limps toward the vehicle.

Tamsen climbs out of her seat, greeting him.

"Fill her up for you–?" the attendant asks, smearing the drool from his lower lip.

She pats her pockets, realizing she's out of change.

"I'll—get you on my way back," she promises him.

The gas attendant rolls his eyes, unconvinced.

Tamsen opens the backseat door and greets Presley as he sits there, fiddling with his polaroid camera.

"I'll be quick. OK?"

Presley merely nods.

Tamsen shuts the door, dashing across the lot—up the porch steps and into the roadside convenience store.

The screen door snaps shut behind her.

She jolts, knocking into novelty toys dangling from the ceiling. She ducks, inching further inside.

Large black flies swarm her. She swats at them and rinses her hands with more hand sanitizer.

The front counter—empty. Beads dangle from a ceiling fan. A small TV arranged in a corner, static washing the screen.

"Hello–? I'm looking for—a headlight?"

She searches the front counter filled with stacks of freshly jarred maple syrup. Scans the racks of newspapers. Her eyes jerk to a headline. She picks up the paper and reads, "Parents blame college student's untimely death on new violent video games."

Tamsen tosses the paper aside.

Without warning, an old woman appears in the doorway. She has the haggard face of an ancient deity. Takes a drag from a cigarette, releases a cloud of smoke from her stoma. Her voice—filled with gravel.

"What do you need–?" she asks.

Tamsen hesitates, cautious. "I—broke one of my headlights. Do you sell replacements?"

The old woman points a crooked finger and turns her head slightly, revealing a black ring stretching a giant hole in her cheek.

"Window cleaners and oil down there," she says, pulling at the whiskers on her chin. "Haven't seen headlights in a while. You can check."

The old woman perches behind the counter, watching.

Tamsen, uneasy, begins to meander down the aisle. She glances out a nearby window as she passes and notices

9

something: a dark grove of trees nestled on the opposite side of the roadway.

Tamsen squints, leaning toward the glass. She sees movement.

Some of the branches stir.

As the undergrowth comes apart, a dark figure rips itself from hiding. The vague outline of its human-like body—an ornate latticework of thin steel wires and dripping wet with black sludge.

Its ragged form—shiny metal filaments like the exposed circulatory system of a body without any muscle or skin.

The creature turns, its head nothing more than a threadbare ball masked with wires.

Without warning, Presley flies into the store, tripping over a wooden pine tree carving and snapping it in half.

"Tam," he shouts.

The old woman reels from her seat, furious.

"You have to pay for that," she barks at him.

But he doesn't hear her.

Presley dashes toward Tamsen but stops short of a hug.

"Pres–?"

The old woman barrels down the aisle with the splintered remains of the pine tree carving.

"It's ten dollars," she says.

Tamsen glares at Presley with mother-like disappointment.

"Presley."

"I'm sorry," he says, shrinking.

Presley seems to search her for forgiveness. The way his mouth pulls downward, the despair flickering in his eyes—she can't stay mad at him.

"Clean slate," she says, exhaling.

Tamsen opens her wallet and finds a ten-dollar bill. Her last one. Sulking, she hands it to the old woman.

The old crone shoves the broken pine tree at Presley. Then, returns to the counter. Tamsen trails her.

"Do you know if there's a place around here that sells car parts?" Tamsen asks.

"Where you headed–?"

"Other side of the mountain," Tamsen says, smoothing the letter from her pocket and checking the address. "Whitefield–?"

"My sister makes monsters," Presley says, peering over the store counter.

Tamsen eyes Presley, as if to say, "Not now."

He shrinks, moving away back down the aisle.

"It's the Zimpago Estate," Tamsen says. "Do you know–?"

Suddenly, Tamsen notices how the old woman seems to slow, her eyes dimming with a glassy film.

"He's waiting for you," the old woman says, her eyes rolling to the back of her head as if lost in a trance. "Only the boy can destroy him."

Without warning, a black centipede crawls out from her stoma, slithers up her throat, and disappears inside her open cheek.

She bites down.

CRUNCH.

The old woman's pupils finally center, as if severed from her trance.

She blows smoke in Tamsen's face and then retreats to the stockroom where she disappears.

Tamsen's mouth hangs open in disbelief.

Her eyes shoot across the counter to the television screen.

On the screen, a middle-aged mother is being interviewed by a well-dressed reporter. The mother wipes her eyes with a handkerchief, her voice trembling when she speaks.

"I'll always blame the video games for what happened to him," the mother says. "They changed him. He wasn't my son anymore."

Tamsen pulls her eyes away.

She sees Presley in the far corner of the store. He's distracted, reading the ingredients to a small box of rice.

Tamsen hesitates, thinking: "Do I dare?"

She swallows hard, finally making the decision, as she tears out of the store. Hastening down the porch steps, she makes a dash toward her car.

The gas attendant circles the hood, eyeing her with confusion.

"Your boy took off running–" he says, scratching his head.

Tamsen pulls at the door handle, throwing herself into the driver's seat and shoving the keys into the ignition as the engine purrs sweetly.

She grips the steering wheel. Ten and two. Then, pushing on the brakes, she grabs the clutch. About to hit the gas.

Suddenly, her eyes snap to the front porch of the convenience store. She sees her little brother standing there—lost, bewildered—as he holds the splintered remains of the pine tree carving.

Sensing the color drain from her face, she realizes she's been caught. Tamsen turns off the car, flinging the door open as she climbs out.

"I—thought I hid some money in the–"

But her voice trails off, nervous. Presley doesn't react.

"Ready?" she asks, her lips creasing with a rehearsed smile.

She goes to open the backseat door, but he already has it opened. He slides inside with the pine tree.

Tamsen lunges into the driver's seat, breath whistling. Adjusts the rearview mirror. Looks at Presley. His eyes avoid her.

She pushes the radio on. A woman's gentle, soothing voice fills the car stereo system.

"Recovering Joy from Grief," the voice announces. "A guide to living a happy and healthy life after the death of a loved one."

Tamsen looks in the rearview mirror, observing Presley as he tinkers with his camera. Her eyes widen when she notices her brother's mouth moving along to every word with the audio.

"Chapter Four: Another Beginning," the woman's voice says. "You deserve another chance. Yes. I mean—you. Some people are afraid of starting over. But not you. Not anymore."

Tamsen shifts the car into gear, easing on the gas. The vehicle ambles out of the lot and drifts into the tree-lined roadway.

What she doesn't seem to notice is how as they drive off, the pavement seems to lift from the ground and rises—disappearing into the air like wisps of smoke.

CHAPTER
THREE

Tamsen's car crawls down a narrow driveway and slows as it nears a massive iron gate. The balusters—roped with steel wires like vines. Stone pillars tower above the small vehicle.

Rusted metal statues of demonic creatures leer at her and Presley from their stone perches.

Tamsen recoils, eyes searching the entrance. She notices Presley stir in the rearview mirror, grimacing as he cowers at the sneering metal sculptures.

"What are they–?" he asks.

"Wait here."

Tamsen opens the door, lifting herself out of her seat, and approaches the main gate. It's then she notices a small panel housing an intercom system buried in black weeds beside the gate. She holds down the "CALL" button.

It rings softly.

Then, a red light appears, blinking.

A woman's voice answers—distorted, mechanical.

"Yes–?"

"Hi. Yes. I'm here to see Mr. Zimpago," Tamsen says,

holding down the button. "I was—uhh—We're working on a project together."

"Your name," the woman's voice replies.

"Tamsen."

"Last name?"

"Deerling. He's—expecting me–"

The gate hums alive, the iron bolt unfastening.

"You'll have to open the gate manually," the woman explains before the intercom's red light disappears.

Tamsen's eyes follow the gate's iron rods to their gilded spikes.

She searches the metal winged sculptures squatting on both stone towers beside the entrance.

Distracted by their grotesque appearances, she pulls the gate open and scrapes her palm against a shard of metal. Crying out, she checks her hand. The wound oozes black oil.

As the gate swings open, it slams against her right headlight. More broken pieces shatter.

"Fuck."

She looks at her hand. The oil—gone. The wound —vanished.

She pushes the gate closed, kneeling beside the already bruised fender. Inspects the new damage—another dent in the bumper and the headlight now completely shattered.

Tamsen looks around, at a loss.

Wind rushes past, whispering all around her.

THE CAR AMBLES UP THE STONE DRIVEWAY AND PULLS UP TO THE main house, circling the small island of greenery arranged with a giant metal sculpture.

The statue kneels, its head—split open like a fresh axe

wound. Hanging from its open mouth as if in mid-retch—a black centipede.

Tamsen's eyes wander from the statue to the colossal house looking down upon them.

A modern-styled French chateau. The steep, pitched towers. The elegant double-paned windows. The imperial-looking oak doorway set inside an arched opening.

Presley peers through the window, aiming his camera.

"This is our new home–?" he asks.

"Do you like it?"

"It's a castle," he says, snapping a picture. His eyes—wide and filled with wonder.

Climbing out of the car, Tamsen can't pull her eyes away from the house.

Just then, the front door opens and a woman wearing a red hijab emerges and immediately greets them.

Tamsen opens the backseat door. Presley climbs out, his camera aiming at the woman as she approaches.

"Miss Deerling?"

Tamsen pulls on her brother's hand. But soon recoils. She frowns, confused. The veins in his wrist feel—hard like cables.

Before she can say something, Presley drags his hand out of hers.

"Yes," Tamsen says, recapturing her composure. "Uhh —Tamsen."

"I'm Nadia. Mr. Zimpago's nurse and housekeeper."

She extends her hand, and they shake. Presley immediately snaps a picture of their handshake. The camera chirps, printing.

"Pres," Tamsen whispers. "Not now."

Nadia smiles at the little boy, noticing his golden costume.

"You brought royalty with you," she says, kneeling to greet him.

"This is my brother, Presley," Tamsen says, pushing Presley closer toward Nadia.

"It's very nice to meet you, Presley," Nadia says with a sincere smile. "We're excited to have you."

Presley bites the tips of his finger, coyly, as he hands Nadia the Polaroid with a sheepish smile.

"I'm sorry, my dear," she says. "I'll have to take that."

Presley's shoulders drop, his head lowering.

"You'll get it back when you leave. I promise."

She holds out her hand. Presley unwraps the camera from his neck and passes it to her. Nadia, then, eyes Tamsen.

"Cellphones too," she says. "No leaks."

Without arguing, Tamsen hands her dead cellphone over to Nadia who pockets it immediately.

"The house is beautiful," Tamsen says. "I thought I'd have to pay a toll on the driveway."

"It should at least be considered a principality. Don't you think–?" Nadia asks. "Seventy-six acres. Ten of them—gardens with flowers imported from Europe and Asia. Then. The house. Twelve bedrooms. Eight baths. A self-contained suite in the attic. I still get lost."

"How long have you worked for Mr. Zimpago?" Tamsen asks.

"I have the lead on you with a day."

"Only a day–?"

Suddenly, Presley pulls at his sister's sleeve and points.

"Who's that?" he asks.

Tamsen and Nadia follow his finger to the house's attic window where they see a dark figure staring down at them, watching. Then, as if called away, the figure withdraws and retreats behind the window curtain.

"That's Mr. Zimpago's sister," Nadia explains. "She lives in the suite upstairs and handles her brother's business."

Her eyes narrow at Tamsen. "She'll want to meet with you once you settle in."

"Yes," Tamsen says, as if remembering. "Our bags."

"Leave them," Nadia says. "I'll give you the tour first. We have a lot of ground to cover."

Nadia guides Tamsen and Presley as they scale the front steps toward the house's massive open doorway.

"Does Edward Rochester live here, too?" Presley says.

"Who, dear?" Nadia asks.

"From *Jane Eyre*," he says.

Tamsen's eyes seem to linger on a statue leering at them from a ledge on the rooftop. The wrought iron figure—an axe raised high above its shoulders and prepared to bring the blade down.

The wind murmurs all around Tamsen, carrying with it the sound of distant voices.

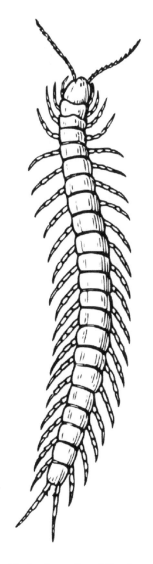

You've lost a lot of blood . . .

I SEARCH FOR YOU UNTIL MY LUNGS SPROUT METAL[1]

I search for you until my lungs sprout metal,
until my hands crisp like rain-soaked parchment,
until I can taste only blood and ash—
both siblings of your exquisite martyrdom.
And in that sadness, I find something lovely,
something to keep me sated while I
think of the man you once were and how
you had once held me like a child's body
to be served as if it were the Holy Eucharist—
a whisper closed off inside a metal sarcophagus,
a mistake once made that can never be unmade.

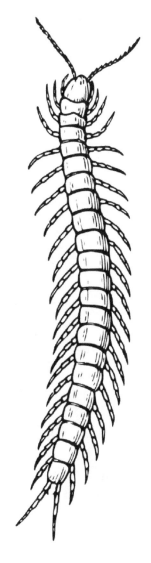

You've lost a lot of blood . . .

STORIES YOU CAN'T TELL AT PARTIES: February 12th, 2019

[The following transcript was recorded on the evening of February 12th, 2019 with Martyr Black's cellphone. The recording was one of the several found among his possessions. The text written in italics was recorded over the original recording by Martyr Black.]

AMBROSE: What are you thinking about?

MARTYR: Killing him.

MARTYR: Nothing.

AMBROSE: You look like you're lost in thought.

MARTYR: I'd rather be lost than be found.

MARTYR: I'm just thinking.

AMBROSE: About our new place?

MARTYR: No. About hurting him.

MARTYR: Something else.

AMBROSE: Tell me.

MARTYR: Go back to sleep.

AMBROSE: Can't sleep. Tell me?

MARTYR: I could do it right now. I could let go of the steering wheel and crash us into one of those trees.

MARTYR: I was just thinking about a story I heard.

AMBROSE: Yes?

MARTYR: It's stuck in my mind.

AMBROSE: That's a funny expression.

MARTYR: Yes?

AMBROSE: Stuck in my mind. Like our brains are made of flypaper and our thoughts are little insects to be captured, caught, and killed.

MARTYR: What a stupid thing to say. It's just an expression.

For Christ's sake, the things he says—the delight he finds in the absurd, the ironic—that's not the reason why I'm going to kill him. In fact, I don't think I've ever really thought about the reason why I've so desperately wanted to hurt him, to watch him suffer. If our brains really are flypaper, then Ambrose would be the biggest horsefly you could imagine—buzzing through the corridors of my mind and building a small nest there.

MARTYR: I was thinking about a story I read online. Somebody had posted about it on one of those chat forums —a place where you can share the most upsetting things you've ever seen.

AMBROSE: Why were you looking there?

MARTYR: Because I like to think about things that upset me.

MARTYR: I don't know. It just seemed to happen. I found this post about this mother who was practically suicidal. Her daughter was turning thirteen and she wanted to surprise her with a birthday cake from her favorite bakery. It was a beautiful cake—vanilla frosting with roses for decoration. But the baker didn't tell the mother that they had inserted these sharp wooden sticks inside the cake because they had built it so high. So, the time came for the daughter to blow out the candles at her birthday party and the mother, without thinking, shoved her daughter's face into the cake—stabbing her in the eye. They rushed her to the hospital, but it was too late to save the poor girl's eye. She's blind now in her left eye. Wears an eye patch—a permanent souvenir of her mother's affection, her mother's playfulness, her mother's terrible mistake.

AMBROSE: How awful.

MARTYR: Yeah.

AMBROSE: I guess that's one story you can't tell at parties.

MARTYR: I don't know about that.

AMBROSE: You don't?

MARTYR: That statement implies that there are, in fact, correct stories to tell at parties. How would you know? You could be entertaining a group of aristocrats. Certainly, they might object to such a gruesome tale. But a colony of lepers wouldn't. In fact, they might praise you for passing along such a yarn.

AMBROSE: But that implies that the lepers are less than the aristocrats.

MARTYR: Aren't they?

AMBROSE: Maybe in some people's eyes. But what about a leprous aristocrat?

MARTYR: No such thing.

AMBROSE: You've never heard of King Baldwin the fourth of Jerusalem.

MARTYR: I haven't.

AMBROSE: One of the few noblemen to suffer from the disease. He developed leprosy when he was very young. Permanently sick throughout the entirety of his ruling, he soon became blind and suffered severe ulceration of the extremities. He might object to your story.

MARTYR: It isn't my story. It's some poor, pathetic woman on the internet. It belongs to her.

AMBROSE: Stories don't belong to people.

MARTYR: If they're published, they do. The certain arrangement of words written down—if I were to publish them, they'd belong to me. If anybody dared to take them from me, recycle them, and reuse them as their own, that's plagiarism.

AMBROSE: True. But I'm talking about oral history— stories that aren't written anywhere, that are mythic, that belong to the mouths that share them. For instance, that story you just told, that became something else when you told it. You could've left out certain information, added what you wanted. Storytelling is an art form, and it belongs to no one.

MARTYR: What's a story you know? Something that upsets you, disturbs you. Something that hasn't been written down. Something that you heard—that merely exists in the minds of those who have heard it.

AMBROSE: It's not something I like to think about.

MARTYR: Pansy. Always deflecting. Even when we're having a conversation that remotely interests me, engages me—he finds a way to deny me what I'm after, what I really want most of all.

MARTYR: Tell me.

AMBROSE: If I tell you, it won't be disturbing.

MARTYR: Why's that?

AMBROSE: I could tell you something disturbing. Tell you a story about a teenager who had his foreskin ripped off during sex and the girl he was with still finished blowing him anyway, blood smearing the poor girl's face. Or tell you a story about a businessman who was paid a hundred dollars to eat fresh bird shit from the hood of his car. They might make you recoil, shrink in disgust when I describe certain things. But I'd unsettle you even more if I chose not to share with you the disturbing story I know. Your mind would invent something even more grotesque, more upsetting than my words could ever conjure.

MARTYR: You're not going to tell me?

AMBROSE: And that's what makes it a truly upsetting story. Think about the film, *The Thing*[1]. Is it as frightening as a more thoughtful and precise effort like *The Haunting*[2]?

MARTYR: I don't see how you can compare the two.

Especially if we're talking about *The Thing* and *The Haunting*. They're two completely separate pieces of art, frightening in their own ways.

AMBROSE: But clearly one is superior. There's something far more unnerving about what you don't see than what you're actually shown. The same fear you experience when you see human bodies twist and curl into absurd abominations isn't the same as when Julie Harris turns on the bedroom lights and wonders whose hand had been holding hers in the dark.

MARTYR: That argument implies that one film is superior to the other.

AMBROSE: Well, of course.

MARTYR: You can't compare the two.

AMBROSE: Of course, you can. One of the films uses provocative and outlandish practical effects to astound and titillate while the other film establishes mood and an overwhelming sense of dread early on to create a truly horrific experience.

MARTYR: So, you're saying that Carpenter's *The Thing* is inferior to *The Haunting*?

AMBROSE: Naturally.

MARTYR: If I showed you something horrible, you'd piss yourself and run screaming.

AMBROSE: But there's something to be said about being far more afraid of what we don't see. It's the same reason some people don't like to swim in the ocean. If we see something truly horrible, immediately we can assess it and recognize its flaws. But to be sidelined by something from beneath the water, to become prey to some ancient deity circling the black depths is something far more serious. Your mind can invent something truly horrible when the monster is kept out of sight. Think of the opening scene in *Jaws*.

MARTYR: I knew you were going to bring that up.

AMBROSE: We never even see the shark attack the poor girl. But our minds invent something far more hideous when the monster is alluded to as opposed to being paraded out in the open.

MARTYR: I like to see the monster. I like to know exactly what I'm dealing with. There's nothing unsettling about not seeing the creature. It's annoying. Besides, most of the time it's done because they can't afford to show the monster.

AMBROSE: That's not always true. Besides, our minds are complex and capable of inventing something far more gruesome from inferences and implications. That's why I'm not telling you the story I'm thinking of. I'm going to let you wonder, to let you consider what it could have been.

MARTYR: So, you're not going to tell me?

AMBROSE: Think about the car we're in right now. If I told you there's somebody sitting in the dark backseat, your eyes might snap to the rearview mirror—you might become unsettled, annoyed that you can't see what I'm seeing.

MARTYR: There's nobody sitting in the backseat.

AMBROSE: That you can see right now. But notice how the light doesn't reach all the way — some of the seat is still dark. In fact, I'd say most of the seat is dark. Someone could easily be sitting there—watching you—and you'd never know. That's more frightening than seeing them there. The possibility of them being there—knowing that they can see you, but you can't see them.

MARTYR: You're goading me.

AMBROSE: You don't like to think about it.

MARTYR: I don't like to think about a lot of things.

AMBROSE: Like what?

MARTYR: Can't tell you. They'd frighten you.

AMBROSE: Touché.

MARTYR: I'll tell you this—they're stories you can't tell at parties.

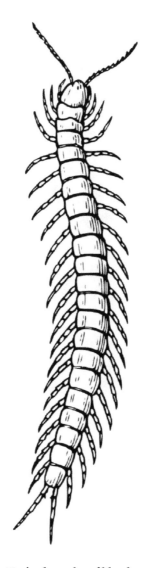

You've lost a lot of blood . . .

YOU'VE LOST A LOT OF BLOOD:

PART TWO

[The following text includes the next three chapters of a novella, You've Lost a Lot of Blood, *that Martyr Black had published by Carter Hill Press in October of 2018.]*

CHAPTER FOUR

Nadia leads Tamsen and Presley into the marble-floored entryway where a giant bust of Abbas Zimpago greets them—a well-coiffed gentleman with an easily frowning mouth and caterpillar-like eyebrows.

Nadia shows Tamsen the finger-print scanner beside the door.

"Every door in the house instantly locks and can only be opened by using these scanners," she explains. "We'll have to take a reading of your fingerprint, so you have access."

Tamsen senses her face scrunch with bewilderment as her eyes come upon a large dent in the wall beside the main entryway.

"Every room is monitored with a security system," Nadia says. "If you try to access an unrestricted area more than three times, you'll set off the emergency system."

Nadia's voice trails off as she lectures, Tamsen's attention following Presley as he seems to notice a few small pink flower petals settling on the marble floor. They glitter, winking at him as if light were being reflected off them.

Presley trails the petals while they scatter at his feet. He chases them until he reaches the grand hall, Tamsen chasing after him.

His eyes follow the glittering blooms as they drift up toward a Japanese cherry tree.

Framed in the glow of the room's skylight, the massive tree drips petals from blossom-gowned branches.

"My favorite room in the house," Nadia says, appearing in the doorway behind brother and sister.

Tamsen, mouth open, approaches the tree.

"This isn't–?"

Her voice trails off.

She reaches out to touch the tree trunk, her fingers passing through a glistening curtain of light—a hologram.

The cherry tree flickers. Then, vanishes as if it were sucked into the drain fixed at the center of the floor.

A giant waterfall replaces the tree, thundering into the room.

A shimmering screen of water cascades at Presley's feet. He lurches back, startled.

"Careful," Nadia says. "It has twelve different settings. Everything from a windmill in the Netherlands to a palm tree in the Amazon. But this one is my favorite."

The water roars, curtains of mist foaming at the floor.

NADIA GUIDES TAMSEN AND PRESLEY INTO THE OFFICE. THE room's centerpiece: a massive desk built from sycamore.

Sunlight streams in from floor-length double-paned doors.

Framed artwork hangs from the walls. A sculpture made of steel stands in the corner like a centurion.

Tamsen notices a familiar poster, moving toward it.

Her eyes scan the gruesome artwork—a small, doll-faced boy crouching on the floor and holding a sinister-looking Jester puppet, the marionette strings made of barbed wire. The poster's title: "Hysteric Puppet 2: The Playroom."

"This is where you'll be working," Nadia says, circling the desk and referring to paperwork. "Mr. Zimpago already cleared you to access the system. You won't have any restrictions. You'll have access to the entire network."

Tamsen approaches the sculpture standing guard in the corner of the room.

The silvery figure appears as if pieces of metal were ripped away during the moment of creation.

She notices a gold plaque fixed at the foot of the sculpture. It reads: "ENGINE."

Peering behind the statue, she finds a silver earring in the shape of a snake discarded on the floor.

She swipes it from the floor and rubs it between her thumb and index finger.

"Yours?" Tamsen asks, glancing at Nadia.

"Maybe Ms. Zimpago's? Thank you, dear."

Tamsen passes the earring to Nadia who hastily pockets it.

Then, Nadia recovers a folder beside the computer monitor and pulls out a sheet of paper.

"A map of the property. The main house on the front side. The gardens are on the back–"

"Where is everyone?" Tamsen asks, glancing around the empty room.

"Everyone–?"

"The other artists," Tamsen says. "I—thought I'd be working with a team."

"There's no one else, dear," Nadia tells her.

Tamsen folds her arms, confused. *How can this be?*

"Do you know—what I'm working on?" she asks.

Nadia frowns, as if afraid Tamsen would ask. She shakes her head, embarrassed.

Tamsen's face scrunches again, confused.

Her eyes latch to another poster. Her face softens, surprised. Mouth opens with soundless words as she approaches the frame.

The poster—a human face sculpted from coils of steel. An ornate mask of metal paired with a headdress of cables. Eyes closed. Mouth open, as if in mid-scream. A thread of black oil creeps from the cable-thin lips.

Tamsen's eyes drift further down the poster until she arrives at the title—YOU'VE LOST A LOT OF BLOOD.

She recoils.

"Is it—this–?" she asks Nadia, shrinking from the poster.

"Some of these could use a sheet draped over them," Nadia says, eyeing the camera mounted on the ceiling. "But I don't think Ms. Zimpago would approve."

Tamsen drifts closer to the artwork, mesmerized.

"I—didn't think it was real," she says.

"What is it?" Nadia asks, as if embarrassed of her ignorance.

"It's a game," Tamsen explains, her eyes coveting the poster's artwork. "One of the first he ever created. But, never released. I heard the system was designed so you could only play the game once. Takes "permadeath" to a whole new level."

"He hired a true fan."

"He's a genius."

Tamsen senses Presley push himself beneath her

armpit. She wraps an arm around him and winces at what her affection really is—a rehearsed imitation of motherhood, a poor substitute for a mother that's no longer there.

"What's it about—?" Presley asks.

"He said it was about—changing. His games are the opposite of entertainment. They're about what the user can do for the game. Not the other way around."

Presley flinches slightly. "Is it scary—?"

"Change is always scary," Tamsen tells him.

Presley's eyes remain glued to the poster. He grimaces.

Nadia taps Tamsen on the shoulder, pulling her eyes away from the poster.

"There's something I was told to show you," she tells her.

CHAPTER FIVE

Nadia leads Tamsen and Presley into the house's artillery chamber.

Sunlight washes the glass cases filled with various weapons. Each instrument—organized and arranged with painstaking finesse.

Tamsen scans the room in wonder-filled disbelief.

"It's—everything from his games," she whispers.

She passes a small display case filled with a giant Medieval-styled axe embellished with a dramatic snake-like handle.

"From the first "Hysteric Puppet" game," she says, pressing her fingers against the glass.

From her peripheral vision, she watches as Presley meanders beside another display case and intently studies a mace with an iron-spiked head in the shape of a human skull.

He seems to wince at the sight.

"Some of these were handmade by fans," Nadia explains. "Others he designed."

Tamsen glides toward a display case, eyes widening as she studies the weapon—a tactical hammer axe.

The handle—sculpted with columns of human skulls, snakes slithering in the open mouths and connecting each head.

The giant blade glints at her in the light.

"I—don't recognize this one," Tamsen says, her eyes searching the axe for an explanation.

"Tam. Look at this," Presley shouts from across the room, severing his sister's concentration.

She turns and notices he's standing in front of a massive wall decorated with rows of masks.

Tamsen follows her brother. She doesn't notice the small bead of blood on the axe's blade.

Presley covets each mask, wide-eyed with wonder.

"Aren't they beautiful–?"

Tamsen scans the wall. Studies each mask. Small golden plaques are fixed on each shelf and feature the title of every game.

Some of the most puzzling—a rubber gimp headpiece in the shape of a Medieval plague doctor mask, a spiked steel skull wrapped with various wires and cables, a gemstone-covered mask with massive copper horns.

"It's every monster from his games," she says. "The doctor from *Sick Bay*. The jester from the *Hysteric Puppet* series."

Tamsen notices one of the shelves is empty. A missing mask. The plaque reads: "You've Lost a Lot of Blood."

"He must've been pleased to hire such a devoted follower," Nadia says.

Tamsen's eyes lower slightly, unsure. "I just—hope he likes me. Do you know when I start?"

"You already have."

"Working with him, I mean."

Nadia pales, as if she had been dreading such inquisitiveness.

"Ms. Zimpago will explain better than I can–"

Although Nadia strains to usher Tamsen and Presley toward the door, Tamsen stalls.

"When can I meet with him–?"

Nadia titters, visibly nervous.

"You can't," she says. "Ms. Zimpago said–"

"How is he supposed to approve my designs if he won't meet with me?"

"It's not that he won't... It's impossible."

Tamsen merely searches Nadia's face for an explanation.

THROUGH A SMALL WINDOW FIXED AT THE CENTER OF THE DOOR, Tamsen peers into the master suite and regards her employer—Abbas Zimpago.

Reclining on an antique sleigh bed, every inch of Zimpago's small body is wrapped with linen bandages as if he were a mummified Pharaoh. His eyes—secreted with black goggles that make him resemble a predatory insect.

An assortment of machines flanks his bedside, tubes snaking through his dressings and attached to his hands and mouth. The devices chirp, monitoring his vitals.

From the corner of her eye, Tamsen notices Nadia studying the bewilderment etched into her face.

"I wasn't told the exact details of the accident," Nadia explains.

"Is he–?"

The question hangs in the air for a moment, far too delicate to answer.

"His sister won't say," Nadia says. "But she made one thing absolutely clear—she doesn't want me or anyone else near him."

Presley's fingers lean on the fingerprint scanner beside the door. The screen blazes red. No match.

"Pres. Don't," Tamsen says, shooing him away from the door.

"She's the only one allowed in the room," Nadia explains.

"If she didn't want someone else looking after her brother, why did she hire a nurse?" Tamsen asks.

Nadia shrugs. Just as bewildered as Tamsen.

Tamsen's eyes return to the window, watching Zimpago's motionless body.

"When can I speak to her?" she asks.

———

TAMSEN SCALES THE STAIRS, REACHING THE LANDING OUTSIDE IRIS' attic suite.

Her reflection flashes at her as she passes an iron-framed mirror fastened to the wall. She does a double-take, noticing a figure looming behind her—another metal sculpture.

This one, larger than the others and outfitted with a pair of steel wings. Unfurled as if prepared to ascend.

An elongated insect-like head embellished with the curled horns of a goat. Eyes and nose—absent. Only a small mouth.

Its face—the front metallic panel extended from the

skull and framed with wires connected to the rim of each wing.

The metal cables—fastened to the creature's lips and securing them to remain open like surgical mouth props.

Tamsen's eyes wander behind the figure. She notices a word carved into the wall—"Engineer."

She doesn't notice the TV screen beside the attic door flicker alive.

Iris Zimpago appears on the screen, seated in an armchair beside a fireplace. Her face—obscured behind a black headpiece. She's dressed in expensive black.

Her voice—pinched and brittle thin, as if pained.

"Miss Deerling–?"

Tamsen jumps, startled.

She squints, peering into the monitor. Notices a priest-like collar belting the old woman's neck. The device blinks a red light at her and moves as she speaks.

"Yes," Tamsen says. "Hi. I'm sorry–"

"Forgive me if our meeting is short. I'm not myself today," Iris says. "Anything you need, Nadia will see to it."

"She said you'd have instructions for me," Tamsen says, hesitant to approach the small screen.

"We expect you to work quickly. That's all."

"And the game I'll be working on. I—was never told–"

"I imagine you've heard the rumors about *You've Lost a Lot of Blood*," the old woman says.

Tamsen's eyes light up.

"He finished it?" she asks.

"The game's been finished for years. Stuck in development hell," Iris explains. "Before his—accident, he and his team overseas had completed the final beta mode of the game."

Iris retrieves a touchscreen device from the small table beside her chair. Her fingers flick across the screen.

"The alpha mode tested poorly with the user we contracted. We've smoothed out the bugs. But, some of the designs are still embarrassing. We've already pushed back the closed beta release date twice."

Iris passes the device through the electronic door slot. Tamsen swipes her fingers across the screen, her face glowing in the monitor's light.

"This is all the information you'll need to complete your new design," Iris says. "All of my brother's notes. Can we count on you to fix our problem?"

Tamsen, obviously overwhelmed, pulls her eyes from the touchscreen and does her best to fake a sales pitch.

"Yes. Absolutely," she assures her. "I –already have some ideas. Illustrations I've been working on. Freelance material. I was hoping I could show you–"

"We need results soon," Iris barks at her. "I'll see to it you're paid extra if you're as efficient as we expect."

"Yes. Of course–"

"When you finish settling in, you can begin work today," Iris says. "I've had Nadia arrange the suite in the East Wing for you."

Tamsen stammers, hesitant to object. "I—was told we'd have more privacy. Your brother's letter mentioned a carriage house?"

Iris pauses, as if visibly annoyed.

"I don't want my brother Presley to disturb you," Tamsen says.

"You'll both have more than enough privacy in the East Wing," Iris says, folding her hands across her lap and turning away.

"I don't think it would be best–"

Tamsen stops herself, as if surprised by her brashness. Iris does not move. Then, after an uncomfortably long pause, the old woman uncrosses her arms.

"Very well," she says. "Nadia will show you to the carriage house. You'll begin work tomorrow morning."

"Thank you. I'm—excited to start."

Iris' eyes narrow at Tamsen with intent. "You should be," she says to her. "This is going to change your life."

CHAPTER SIX

After Nadia tours Tamsen and Presley through the remainder of the house, she guides them out to the small carriage house on the opposite end of the causeway—a small French-styled chateau tucked beside the forest's edge.

Tamsen's car idles in front of the flower-gowned pathway as she and Nadia unload the baggage from the trunk.

Presley loiters nearby, folding the property map into the shape of a small bird.

Clouds begin to gather, hiding sunlight. The wind murmurs, a storm brewing.

"You'll be much happier here," Nadia says, slipping a set of keys into Tamsen's hands. "No fingerprint scanners or holograms. It's like the Middle Ages."

Tamsen drags her suitcase around the corner of the car, eyes looking everywhere but where she's walking.

"It's perfect–"

Just then, a stream of fire shoots at her feet.

She jumps back, screaming.

"Shit."

A young woman kneels in front of her, aiming a blow-torch at the weed-cracked pathway. She's tall, broad shoul-dered, and attractive enough to make Tamsen feel uncomfortable.

She straightens, yanking earbuds from her ears. Her impish grin softens to remorse.

"Sorry," she says. "I—didn't see you–"

They stare at each other for a moment. Smiles break between them. Tamsen begins to laugh.

The young woman relaxes, pleased she's not upset. She lowers the blowtorch.

"Your feet looked a little cold," she teases.

"Most people offer a handshake," Tamsen says. "Not third-degree burns."

"Oh, good. Dani, will you help us?" Nadia asks the young woman. "This is the new game developer. Miss Deerling."

"Tamsen," she says, offering her hand.

They shake, holding hands perhaps for a second too long.

"The monster maker," Dani says. "I pictured you arriving in a hearse."

"One more step and I would've been leaving in one," Tamsen jokes.

Presley ambushes his sister, revealing the map he's folded into a swan.

"Look what I made."

Tamsen deflates at the reminder.

"This is my brother Presley," she says, pushing him toward Dani.

"Nice to meet you, King," Dani says, shaking the boy's hand.

Presley's eyes light up. "You know Elvis–?"

"Who doesn't know the King of Rock 'n roll?"

Presley flashes a scowl at his sister. "Tamsen hates him."

Color fills Tamsen's cheeks. She crosses her arms, embarrassed. "I do not hate him."

"She hates everything Dad used to love," Presley says.

"Pres," Tamsen says.

But there's nothing else she can think to say. After all, she knows full well he's right.

"Dani, will you show these two inside?" Nadia asks. "I have to get back."

"Thank you for everything," Tamsen says quietly.

Nadia cups Tamsen's hands in her own. "You let me know if you need anything."

Then, she pinches Presley's cheek. "Both of you."

Nadia heads off on the driveway toward the main house.

Dani grabs the suitcases, ushering Tamsen and Presley up the pathway and toward the carriage house's front door.

"I've never met a "Tamsen" before," Dani says.

"It's from an Aramaic word," Presley explains. "It means *twin*."

"Aramaic. That's a big word for a little guy."

"He knows more. Believe me," Tamsen says. "What's the word of the day, Pres?"

"Verisimilitude," the boy says, as they filter inside the house. "The appearance of being true or real."

———

As Presley unpacks his suitcase in the room next door, Dani drags some of Tamsen's bags into her bedroom.

"Did you know Mr. Zimpago before the accident?" Tamsen asks her.

Dani looks at Tamsen for instructions regarding her suitcase.

Tamsen merely gestures and Dani hurls the luggage on the bed.

"No. Never met him," she says. "Only met with his sister once."

Tamsen starts to unpack.

"Does she always wear those–?"

"In the day I've known her," Dani says, shrugging.

As Tamsen reaches for another wire hanger in the closet, she stops. Head tilting, eyes cramp with confusion.

She pulls out a sweatshirt.

"Did I—already hang this?"

She turns, noticing Dani staring.

Caught, her eyes avoid her.

"Nadia wanted me to show you how to arm the security system downstairs," Dani says, lowering her head and slipping out of the room.

Tamsen's eyes return to the sweatshirt. Shaking her head, she hangs it in the closet and follows Dani downstairs into the kitchen where the security panel is.

"It doesn't set automatically like the alarms in the main house," Dani explains. "It's already been programmed with a passcode, but you can change it to something you'll remember."

"What's the code?" Tamsen asks.

Dani refers to a small, crumpled piece of paper from her pocket.

"08-14."

"August 14th. That's my birthday."

"There. You won't forget it," Dani says, passing the

paper to her. "There's a phone in the living room. Dial "1" to be connected to the main house."

Dani starts to head for the door. She kneels and picks up a wicker basket filled with a bushel of freshly cut flowers.

"I'll be around if you need anything," she says.

"The nearest market?" Tamsen asks. "Presley can't drink milk. I have to buy him–"

"Check the fridge," Dani says.

Tamsen opens the refrigerator and finds each shelf stocked with fresh produce. She locates a carton of almond milk.

"She sent me to the store this morning."

Tamsen shakes her head in disbelief. "But she had planned for us to stay in the main house. How did she–?"

"Oh. I almost forgot."

Dani sails over to the cabinet filled with stacks of spices and perishables. She moves some cans aside and finds an empty vase. Holds it under the faucet and fills it up.

"Just picked these," she says.

Scoops out some of the flowers from her basket and arranges them in the vase.

Tamsen pales at the sight, uncomfortable.

"Thought you might like them," Dani says. "Make the room a little brighter?"

Tamsen recoils, apprehensive. Unsure what to say.

"Thank you," she says as politely as she can muster. "I have a lot to unpack and I'm—tired from the drive. I don't want to be–"

Dani stammers, embarrassed for clearly overstaying her welcome. "Sure. Yeah, of course. I'll—leave you to it."

Tamsen watches Dani leave until she's out of sight. Her eyes drift to the flowers in the vase, her face filling with dread.

She grabs the flowers, shoving them in the nearby waste bin.

Tamsen searches the cabinets. She opens the pantry. Shrinks at the unwelcome sight—a shelf filled with unopened bottles of liquor.

She hesitates for a moment. Finally, makes the decision:

Tamsen pulls each bottle off the shelf. Rips each cap off. Pours each bottle down the drain.

When finished, her eyes scan the empty shelf. Sees an unopened bottle of vodka tucked behind a box of cake mix. She reaches for it. But it's too far away.

Pulling a chair from the kitchen table, she leans it against the counter. Before she lifts herself up, she stops.

Returns the chair to the table. Closes the pantry.

She sits at the kitchen table.

Face washed in light, her fingers flick across the touchscreen device Iris had given her.

On the screen, an electronic scan of a page filled with chicken-scratch notes stares back at her. The text: "Filled with the capriciousness of his preferred youthful prey, only unspoiled innocence can destroy Him."

Beside the text, a drawing of the same wire-veined winged statue guarding the attic door. A single word beneath the illustration—"Engineer."

Tamsen's eyes remain fixed on the illustration.

She picks up the phone beside her. Dials "1" and waits.

Greeted with deafening silence.

She hesitates. Then, winces. A metallic shriek answers her.

She slams the phone down.

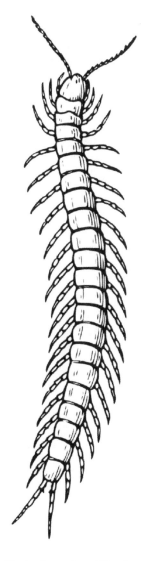

You've lost a lot of blood . . .

TOOTHPICK

It's hard not to wonder
what horrible secrets you
keep hidden away, what
fanged monstrosities you
nurture in your despair.
I wonder if you'll show me
as I take the little toothpick
I've swiped from your nightstand
and push it further inside your
ear until it's gone, a bubble of
blood beading there as if it
were a confession—a horrible
admission of guilt of all
the things you never shared with me.
I feed you the broken bits of
glass from a lightbulb I once
crushed between my hands—
you chew, blood trickling from
between your lips and ask me if
there's any more to be eaten.
I think there's a small, quiet part of
you that enjoys the misery I
carefully feed you each day—
as if it were the very thing keeping you alive.

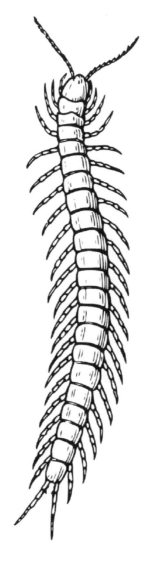

You've lost a lot of blood . . .

I'D DROWN YOU IN DARK WATER IF YOU WEREN'T SO BEAUTIFUL: March 9ᵗʰ, 2018

"I'd drown you in dark water if you weren't so beautiful," I tell the young man before I slit his throat with the small pocketknife I had been hiding. It's a family heirloom my father had given to me when I was a boy because he knew I was far too sensitive for my kind, and he so desperately wanted to correct that behavior—so desperately wanted to drag out the red weed rooted deep inside me that had made his only son a faggot.

I often wondered if he thought of me, my face buried between another man's legs—if he had shuddered to think of his precious boy being taken and passed from gentleman to gentleman in the club bathroom. Perhaps it had tortured him often—to know that the boy he had raised was an abomination, an insect to be squished. The way he had looked at me when I had told him what I was, what I wanted to be, seemed to tell me everything—to him, I was a disgrace: a horrific mistake that he would never make ever again.

The first young man I had ever killed was named Carlos —a young Hispanic boy from Chelsea, MA with dark brown eyes and a mouth that easily frowned. He had been standing out in front of the bodega on Hinkley Avenue and his eyes lingered on me for a beat far too long—an invitation, something I knew he wanted, a soundless message that is only understood between two men. He asked me for a cigarette at first, but the way he seemed to wet his lips and draw out every other word as if in an effort to keep me there longer seemed a shameless display to attract my attention.

I could have reprimanded him for the way he didn't seem to know which piece of silverware to use when room service came. I could have easily sent him on his way when he confessed to being inexperienced in the art of lovemaking, oral sex his preferred method of pleasure and all other opportunities withheld. But there was something so charming about the young man—something I so desperately needed to possess.

I can so distinctly recall thinking how drowning him would have been such an insult to his beauty. For such a young man, he had grown into his features nicely—a handsomely tapered jawline, dark hair smoothed back with gel, and a beauty mark beneath his nose. Some might think that drowning might be far preferable than to have your throat slit. But that must be addressed as false. Although drowning might be peaceful—gently being lulled to sleep as if in the cradle of some underwater God—the aftermath of drowning is unsavory at best. Bodies become bloated, skin prunes like expired fruit discarded in sunlight. Such brutalities would be an insult to this poor boy. Even if it wasn't his intended time to die, I knew I had to make it so.

With a flick of my wrist, I slash at his throat with the pocketknife and watch as blood as black as oil slowly creeps from the ribbon I've opened there. Before too long it's a deluge, a geyser spraying me all over until I'm drenched in his blood—the warm, coppery scent sticking to me as if it were tree sap. As he lays there, his hands gently twitching and his throat leaking more blood, I can't help but think how he resembles a distinguished Russian aristocrat from an era now long since gone. Perhaps a Tsar or a Grand Duke with a dark red scarf draped around his neck—a scarf I've arranged there, a handsome blood-red pashmina to compliment his looks.

This is how I'll remember him—a beautiful boy with an artery-red scarf tightening about his throat. I could pretend to mourn. I could pretend to feign horror at what I've done —the life I've taken, the human I've irreversibly destroyed. But I feel nothing. I could lie to you and tell you I think of his mother—how she'll weep for him knowing her son died alone and afraid, his pants wrapped around his ankles and his hand permanently fastened to his pathetic erection. I could lie and say I think of what he was like as a child—the joy he had brought to his family. But I don't think of any of those things.

Instead, I marvel at my creation—the grotesque artwork I've made with his body as my canvas, his blood as my oils. I don't mourn for him. He's achieved something far greater than what was originally his purpose when standing in front of the bodega on the street in Chelsea.

As is what's now known as my custom, I slice off his index finger and work the wet gristle from the bone until it's completely stripped of flesh. There's apparently a word for that. There's a word for everything, after all. *Excarnation.* It's common in anthropological circles and details the act of removing flesh from the dead before burial. However, I have no intention of burying my protégé. Instead, I intend to leave him there and take a piece of him with me when I leave—his index finger.

When I leave the room, I bury him in my thoughts— he's wrapped in hemlock and ivy until it smothers him, vines creeping from between his lips. That's how I want to remember him. After all, it would have been such a waste to bury him in deep water—to let him float out to sea and be pecked at by fish and different kinds of birds. Perhaps I'll drown one of the others. Yes, I'd be only too glad to find a young man worth drowning.

But not this one.
Anyone but this one.

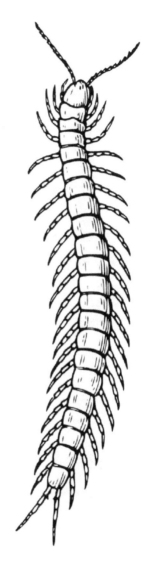

You've lost a lot of blood . . .

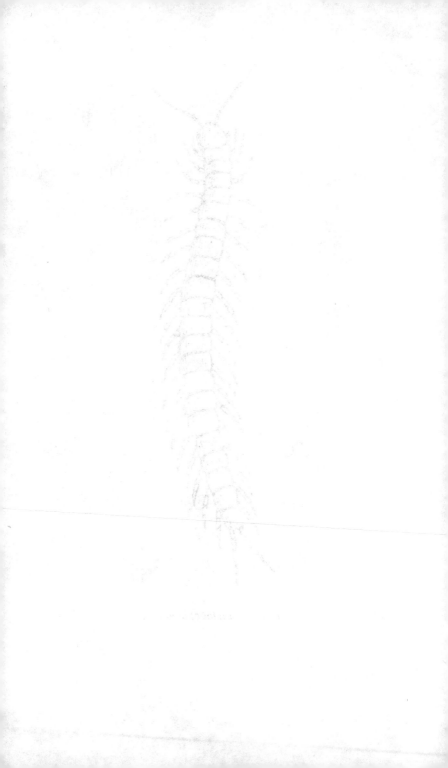

YOU'VE LOST A LOT OF BLOOD:

PART THREE

[The following text includes the next two chapters of a novella, You've Lost a Lot of Blood, *that Martyr Black had published by Carter Hill Press in October of 2018.]*

CHAPTER SEVEN

Later that night, Presley, dressed in pajamas, climbs into bed. Tamsen kneels beside him, combing strands of hair from his face.

"Brush your teeth?" she asks.

He nods.

Tamsen pulls sheets over him. Then, straightens. Feels something beneath the covers. Pulls them back. Finds a book clutched in his hands.

She tears it from his grasp.

"You'll never sleep."

"Five more minutes," he begs her.

Tamsen hides the book behind her back. "You can have it back tomorrow."

Presley winces. He stirs, uncomfortable.

"What's wrong?" she asks him.

"Head hurts," Presley says.

Tamsen softens, cupping her brother's cheek.

"I told you not to read before bed."

"That's why Mom always read to me," he says. "Will you–?"

Tamsen pales, as if she had been dreading the request.

"Maybe tomorrow night," she says, quietly hoping he might forget.

She reaches to switch off the lamp beside Presley's bed. Presley looks at her, distrustful. Expecting the worst.

"If I need you. You'll come back–?"

Tamsen hesitates, unsure how to answer. She forces a smile, grabbing his hand.

"In a second," she says.

Presley pulls his hand out of Tamsen's. "You won't leave me–?"

"You think I'd ever leave you–?"

Tamsen's face flushes with instant regret at the question.

Presley's eyes lower, lip pulling down at the unspoken reminder. He rolls over on his side, turning away.

Tamsen leans in, pecking him on the neck. "Night, Pres."

But he doesn't respond.

She grabs the touchscreen device Iris had given her from the nightstand. Then, switches off the lamp beside the bed.

Darkness swallows the little room.

Standing in the open doorway, Tamsen glances back at Presley one last time. Then, shuts the door.

Retreating downstairs to the kitchen, Tamsen wipes her eyes. She tows the chair in front of the pantry.

Scaling the seat, she opens the cabinet and snatches the bottle of vodka from the shelf.

She crawls down. Twists open the bottle. And takes a gulp.

Then, another. And another.

She crouches on the floor, hugging the bottle.

When she's finished, she stumbles back upstairs to her bedroom. Tamsen, gripping the half-empty bottle of vodka, opens the door. Greeted by a dark room, her hands frisk the wall for the light switch. She can't find it.

Inching further inside, she scans the room. Hands swat the air as if she were blind.

Patting the wall again, her fingers find the light switch. She flicks it on.

A panel of fluorescent lights whir alive, washing the room in an emerald glow.

Tamsen rubs her eyes in disbelief at the sight.

Her bedroom has transformed into—an empty laundromat.

Rows of humming washing machines stretch in front of her.

Shoes clicking as she creeps across the tiles, her reflection flashes at her in the mirror of every washing machine door.

Eyes snap to the empty machine waiting at the end of the aisle, its door creaking open with a wordless invitation.

She notices Presley's polaroid camera discarded beside an empty laundry cart.

The faint murmur of whispering. She looks around, worried.

"Pres–?"

Lights flicker overhead. The panel hums like a beehive.

Something stirs inside the washing machine.

Tamsen recoils, bending down and peering inside.

She sees a dark shape crouching. It unfurls, peeling itself from inside the empty drum. Its edges glimmer.

The shape chirps as it stirs awake.

Tamsen squints, blinking.

70

A thin silver filament uncoils from deep within the machine and curls toward her.

Tamsen feels the pulse of her heart beating in her throat. She swallows, nervous.

About to take another step further when –

A livid screech. Metal grinding against metal.

The creature explodes from its hiding place.

Wires burst from inside the drum, clapping against the door and spiderwebbing across the other washers.

Tamsen screams, slamming the bedroom door shut and hastening down the hallway toward Presley's room.

She flies into her little brother's room, locking the door.

Presley jolts up from sleep, scared.

"Tam?" he calls to her.

Tamsen dashes over to him, the bottle slipping from her hands and shattering on the floor.

"It's OK," she says, nearly retching. "Go back to sleep."

"What happened–?"

She climbs into bed, panting.

"Just do as I say, Pres," she barks at him. "Go to sleep."

Confused, Presley lowers his head. He trembles, dragging the sheets over his head. Tamsen pulls herself closer to him, rolling on her side.

She shakes, eyes darting to the door. Her ears pin at every sound for the rest of the night.

———

THE FOLLOWING MORNING, TAMSEN STIRS, AWAKE. STRETCHES HER arms.

Rubs her head. Another pounding headache.

Her eyelids flutter open.

Rain beats hard against the window.

She lifts her head and finds Presley kneeling on the floor beside the shattered remains of the empty vodka bottle.

He sweeps the broken glass with a broom, collecting the bits in a dustpan.

"Pres–?"

Presley looks up from his labor. Doesn't say anything. Throws her a sour look.

Tamsen leans over the side of the bed. Looks down.

Notices a pool of vomit on the floor, regurgitated flecks dripping down the length of the mattress.

She glances at the alarm clock on the nightstand.

The time: 10:36 am.

"Shit," she says, leaping out of bed.

She hoists a pair of jeans around her waist. Presley watches without comment.

"Why didn't you wake me–?" she asks him.

Just then, the downstairs doorbell chimes.

Tamsen freezes. Horrified.

She scampers downstairs and arrives at the front door where she's greeted by Nadia's cheerful smile.

Dressed in a raincoat, Nadia carries a covered tray. She lifts the platter's lid, revealing an assortment of freshly baked morning pastries.

"I hope you're hungry," she says, pushing past Tamsen and gliding into the foyer.

"I'm so sorry," Tamsen says.

"For what, dear?"

"I—never oversleep. I promise. It won't ever happen again."

"Of course, dear," Nadia says.

"Is she angry–?"

"She wanted to make certain you and your brother were well fed for your first day at work."

Tamsen follows Nadia as they move into the living room.

Presley appears at the foot of the stairs. Sees the tray of baked goods. Eyes widen, hungry and excited.

Nadia sets the platter on the walnut credenza.

"Presley, dear. Have as much as you like," Nadia says. "We'll soon fatten your waifish looks."

Presley scours the plate, licking his lips. Picks a blueberry scone. Sits on the divan and eats.

Nadia tilts the platter toward Tamsen.

"Breakfast wasn't the only reason I came," Nadia explains. "She asked me to extend an invitation to Presley."

Presley's chewing slows. He glances up.

"To the library?"

"Maybe later, dear," Nadia says.

"I—don't understand. An invitation to Presley for what?"

Nadia looks around the room, as if priming her mind for the words she's apparently already rehearsed. "Something she'd like to show him."

"I really should join you, then," Tamsen says. She pulls Nadia closer, whispering. "He tends to wander, and I really shouldn't let him out of my sight."

"She's expecting you to begin your work today, my dear," Nadia tells her.

"Then, Presley can come with me," Tamsen says, folding her arms. "Or I can tell her myself."

Realizing she's not going to win the argument, Nadia deflates slightly. "Very well."

Meanwhile, Presley swipes another blueberry scone from the platter.

73

Outfitted in a Bogart-like trench coat, Presley bounds down the front steps of the carriage house after Nadia. He carries the small origami swan he made.

Tamsen pulls the front door shut, locking it.

She does a double-take, noticing Dani approaching with a dirt-caked shovel.

Nadia and Presley greet her on the driveway.

"I thought she gave you the day off," Nadia says to her.

Tamsen notices Presley tuck the swan inside his pocket.

"Perfect day for digging," Dani says. "She wants the oleander moved from the nursery."

Presley pulls on Nadia's coat. "Can Dani come with us—?"

"Where are you headed?" Dani asks.

Nadia smiles, tight-lipped.

Tamsen descends the steps, pocketing the house key.

"She won't tell us," she says.

Presley grabs Dani's hand, pulling.

"Please, Dani," Presley begs, pulling harder on Dani's arm. "You have to."

Presley pulls harder on Dani's arm.

"I don't have much of a choice," Dani says, tossing her shovel aside.

She smiles, as if pleased to be kidnapped.

Yanking on Dani's arm, Presley hauls her toward the forest as Nadia and Tamsen follow close behind.

CHAPTER EIGHT

Nadia leads Tamsen, Presley, and Dani down the narrow pathway, meandering through the grove of towering oak and pine.

They pull their hoods up as another rainstorm sprinkles down from the emerald canopy above.

Dani eyes Tamsen with a solicitation. She ignores it, keeping her distance from her.

Presley sprints ahead of the group, climbing over a small sapling blocking the path.

"Pres, slow," Tamsen calls after him.

She looks to Nadia, at a loss. "I've never seen him run to anything except a library."

Nadia chuckles, moving ahead.

Presley darts up a hill and looks out into the distance.

"Look at this," he shouts back to the group.

Tamsen scales the ridge, catching up to her brother.

Looking out into the clearing, her eyes widen when she sees it—a giant warehouse.

A manmade alien to its natural surroundings.

The building dwarfs the nearby tree-line like the abandoned remains of a derelict aircraft.

The gargantuan concrete structure—laced with ribbons of greenery.

The building's only entrance—a colossal steel-reinforced doorway with panels of windows.

Presley scampers down the hill, darting into the clearing.

"Pres, wait," Tamsen calls to him.

But he's much too quick for her and already halfway to the building's massive entrance.

Nadia appears beside Tamsen, seeming to savor her bewildered expression.

"This—wasn't on the map," Tamsen says.

They weave through the field of tall grass, mere miniatures approaching the massive structure.

Tamsen notices a dirt road cutting through the forest and ribboning toward the hanger's entrance.

"What have they got in there?" Dani asks. "Nukes?"

Presley leans against the window-paned door, peering inside. Meanwhile, Tamsen looks to Nadia for an answer.

"What is it–?" she asks.

"It's called "The Silo." Mr. Zimpago had it built to house his private gaming center."

Tamsen's eyes drift from the building's concrete colonnade to the steel-pitched roof.

She notices an unusual symbol carved into the exterior.

"I know this marking–"

Presses her hands against it. Recoils, as if in sudden agony. Rubs her head.

"It's—from *You've Lost a Lot of Blood*," she says.

Dani grips the handle and lifts the door open. It buckles, screeching as it flies up.

"Nobody's home," she says, shrugging her shoulders.

They file inside.

Sunlight glitters in the dust-filled air.

Vaulted ceilings latticed with ornate piping and electrical equipment. Aisles organized with inactive machinery—furnaces, boilers, generators.

Presley meanders down the machine-flanked corridor, eyes searching every inch of the facility as if he were the first visitor to an uncharted planet.

Human faces sculpted from metal leer at him from the ceiling's complex maze of wiring and machinery.

Tamsen follows close behind, noticing another symbol drawn in black spray paint on the side of a generator.

Dani brushes past, startling her.

Tamsen looks up. Chains sway from the scaffolding, creaking.

She scans every inch of the room, eyes filled with wonder.

"It's—a replica of the game," she says.

Presley nears the mouth of a stairwell leading down to a dimly lit lower level.

"There's something down there!"

He disappears down the stairs.

"Pres," Tamsen calls to him.

Tamsen and the others chase after him.

Dashing down the steps, Presley reaches the facility's dimly lit lower level.

Nadia flicks on a light switch.

An overhead panel of lights hums alive, bathing the concrete netherworld in a ghostly white glow.

A vacant concrete-walled room with a low ceiling. Two sliding steel doors face one another, framed on opposite sides of the room. An elaborate holographic control panel is thrown against the wall beside each door.

Tamsen descends the stairs, drifting into the room. Nadia and Dani follow close behind.

"She told me it's behind those doors," Nadia explains to Tamsen.

"What–?"

"The thing she wanted to show Presley."

Presley slides the steel door open and inches into the first isolation chamber.

A pitch-black cell with a vaulted ceiling. The walls– shimmering as if slick with streaks of oil. They ripple as if made from viscous, organic-looking material.

The room's centerpiece—the hive.

A massive mechanical device rotates on a small island accessible only by an illuminated gangplank. A leather-cushioned, body-shaped vessel fills the interior of the machine's frame, outfitted with various restraints.

Tamsen enters, Nadia and Dani trailing her.

She scales the small bridge, nearing the monstrous device. Looks down and sees liquid as thick and as black as oil circulating in the moat surrounding the elevated platform.

Presley follows, mesmerized.

"I've heard of these," Tamsen says.

Presley reaches out, pinching one of the harnesses.

"What is it–?"

"It's called a "Hive." A fully immersive VR simulator."

Tamsen's eyes wander to the insignia etched inside the mechanism's steel scaffolding—Zimpago.

Then, she notices an outlet fixed near the cushioned leather headrest inside the vessel. A valve filled with wires connects to a small USB device.

She reads the tiny words printed along the rim of the instrument—YOU'VE LOST A LOT OF BLOOD.

"How does it work?" Dani asks.

Presley slides the doors apart, climbing inside the vessel.

"Pres, get out of there," Tamsen says.

He shifts himself onto the cushioned seat, fastening a belt around his waist.

"I want to play the game," he says.

"Since when?"

Presley slides his arms and legs inside the restraint braces surrounding the chair.

"It's my turn."

"For what–?"

"To leave you."

Tamsen crumples as if his words had pierced through her. She thinks. A compromise:

"I'll go with you."

"No."

She glances at Nadia and Dani, humiliated. Then, back to Presley.

"I don't want you in the simulation by yourself."

"I can go in with him," Nadia offers. "There's another chamber."

Tamsen pulls Nadia aside. Presley leans out of his seat, listening.

"He might get scared," Tamsen says. "He'll panic. You won't know how to help him–"

"I don't want you to come," Presley shouts at her.

"Presley–"

"I want Nadia."

Tamsen looks at Nadia, at a loss. Nadia cups her hands with motherlike tenderness.

"I'll look after him," she assures her. "I promise."

Tamsen approaches her caged brother. "Five minutes. Then I'm turning it off."

Presley doesn't react. Stares her down.

Tamsen slides a transparent helmet over his head. Lighted arteries of wiring snake through the headpiece as it comes alive, connecting to the USB.

She pulls on his restraints, reviewing his safety.

Tamsen can't bear to pull herself away, her sparkling wet eyes offering a soundless "I'm sorry" he doesn't accept.

Head lowering with defeat, she leads Nadia and Dani out of the room and back into the: lower level.

Tamsen drags the steel door shut. Consulting with the control panel beside the chamber, she locates a large red button on the keyboard—LAUNCH SIM.

The door buzzes, a steel latch bolting the door shut.

The light above the door flashes from red to green.

A small touchscreen fixed beside the door flickers on, displaying the animated outline of a human body. Text generates beside the animation, listing Presley's vitals as he experiences the simulation.

Tamsen looks to Nadia.

"Your turn," she says to her.

Tamsen leads Nadia into the second isolation chamber.

The same type of chamber hosting the same giant apparatus.

Nadia climbs into the vessel, Tamsen restraining her.

When finished, she returns to the lower level.

Tamsen pulls the door shut and presses the holographic LAUNCH SIM button on the control panel, the entryway's light flashing green.

Another touchscreen comes alive, displaying Nadia's vitals as she begins the simulation.

Tamsen eyes a large red button on the control panel's keyboard—END SIM.

Her fingers hover, threatening to push down.

"They'll be fine," Dani says.

Tamsen shifts, uncomfortable, as Dani approaches her. She can scarcely speak.

"He's never... He looked at me—like he hated me."

Dani pouts. Glum.

"I know the feeling," she says.

Tamsen searches her face for an explanation.

"Are you allergic to them?" Dani asks.

"What–?"

"The flowers."

Tamsen retreats, embarrassed.

"You looked at me like I was trying to poison you," Dani says. "I saw you threw them out."

"I just–"

"I wasn't trying to make a move or anything," Dani assures her.

"I just don't like flowers," Tamsen says, her eyes lowering. "They remind me of hospitals... Visiting my mom..."

Dani realizes, shrinking.

"I'm sorry... What happened–?"

The unspoken final word of her question hangs in the air. Tamsen rubs her head, pained. Another headache.

"A year ago, my mom and dad were driving to pick up Presley from the library. A tractor trailer spun out on the highway and crashed into them. Dad—died before paramedics got there. Mom lived in the hospital for three days after..."

Dani's eyes lower. "I'm so sorry."

"I kept saying—if it wasn't for him, they wouldn't have been driving."

81

Dani's face scrunches, confused. "You kept saying–?"

"That's what Presley said."

"You said you kept saying..."

Tamsen's face heats red, nervous.

"I—meant Presley," she says. "He kept repeating that. He kept blaming himself–"

"That's not what you thought–?"

"No. I meant to say "Presley." That's what he thought. I never–"

Suddenly, the screen beside Nadia's chamber door blazes red.

The animated outline of her body flickers as text appears across the image—ERROR. Skull and crossbones.

The light above the door flashes red. An alarm pulses.

"Shit," Tamsen says.

Tamsen darts to the screen, searching for an answer.

Text flashes at her—SYSTEM MALFUNCTION.

She reviews the keyboard. Presses "END SIM." No response.

TAPS it again. Nothing. And again. It screeches at her.

"I can't override it."

Dani tries to pull the door's latch. Won't budge.

Tamsen's eyes widen with horror as she notices the screen beside Presley's chamber door burning red. Text appears on the screen, blinking at her—SYSTEM FAILURE.

"Oh my god."

Tamsen pounds on the keyboard. END SIM. No response. She pushes on the door's latch, screaming.

"Go call for help," she hollers at Dani.

Without hesitation, Dani sprints up the stairwell, vanishing out of sight.

Tamsen returns to the control panel, fingers pounding against the keyboard.

The flashing red light above Nadia's chamber turns green, the alarm muted. The touchscreen beside the door goes dark, the steel bolt retracting as the door slides open.

Tamsen watches, frozen, as Nadia staggers into the light.

She's dripping wet with black sludge.

Nadia wipes away the strands of hair glued to her forehead with thick ropes of oil. Doubles over and vomits.

Knees buckling, she crashes to the floor.

Tamsen rushes to her, propping her against the wall.

"What happened–?"

Nadia's head bobs back and forth, groggy. Her lips move with soundless words.

Tamsen recoils at the greasy touch of Nadia's oil-soaked arm.

"What is this–?"

Tamsen looks up - the light above Presley's door flashes green. The latch snaps open, the door sliding out.

"Pres."

Abandoning Nadia, she sprints into the first isolation chamber.

She freezes, covering her mouth as she looks at the Hive —empty.

She races up the gangplank and circles the giant mechanism. Scans the device for a sign of her brother. Nothing.

The vessel's restraints - dangling loose.

"Presley," she screams, choking on sobs. Helpless.

She paces the chamber like a frightened animal.

The small touchscreen beside the door flickers alive. Blinks—INITIATE SIMULATION?

Black sludge creeps across the tiled floor as if it were blood.

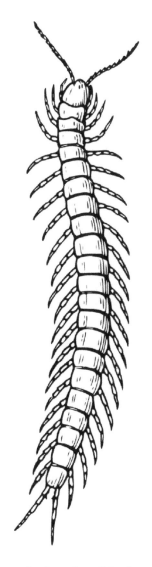

You've lost a lot of blood . . .

TOMB_GIRL_gif: March 10th, 2019

[The following transcript was recorded on the evening of March 10th, 2019 with Martyr Black's cellphone. The recording was one of the several found among his possessions. The text written in italics was recorded over the original recording by Martyr Black.]

MARTYR: "You've lost a lot of blood," I'll say to him, doing my best to contain my glee, my delight in his misery. Knowing him, he'll question me. "Well, how do you know exactly?" he might ask me. "It's all over the floor," I'll tell him. "Streaks of red on white tile." Yes, white tile. Perhaps I'll kill him in the bathroom. After all, there's something so deliciously macabre about red streaks on immaculately polished white tile—something so operatic and decadently grim about the sight of blood curling on a well-polished floor, little threads spiraling into cracks and cooling there. There's something so graceful, so delicate about witnessing the human body welcome death, whether willingly or not as they furiously spray the floor with their final masterpiece: their blood.

AMBROSE: What are you thinking about?

MARTYR: Nothing.

AMBROSE: Didn't seem like nothing.

MARTYR: Seem?

AMBROSE: You had this look on your face.

MARTYR: Yes. Annoyance probably.

MARTYR: Yes?

AMBROSE: It was a thinking look.

MARTYR: I guess.

AMBROSE: You're thinking about him.

MARTYR: What's there to think about? He's dead.

AMBROSE: You weren't thinking about him?

MARTYR: I was thinking of something else. Someone else.

AMBROSE: Tell me.

MARTYR: Did you ever hear the one about the chick they called "Tomb Girl?"

AMBROSE: No.

MARTYR: She couldn't have been older than nineteen or twenty. Met this gentleman at a bar one night and he promised her he'd give her what she was after.

AMBROSE: Yes?

MARTYR: What else? The girl was an addict. So, she followed him home and they had a few drinks, talked for a couple hours. She was lonely. Might have been looking to score some H, but more than anything she was after companionship—someone to call a friend. So, he plied her with liquor and before she knew it, she was being guided down into the basement.

AMBROSE: Why does every scary story involve a basement? It's insulting.

MARTYR: It's not insulting.

AMBROSE: How many horrible movies from the 1980's had something horrible lurking in the basement? There's a film literally called *Don't Look in the Basement*[1].

MARTYR: That wasn't from the 80's. That was released in 1973.

AMBROSE: Excuse me.

MARTYR: This isn't supposed to be a scary story. It's supposed to be disturbing. There's a difference.

AMBROSE: Can't something that disturbs you also scare you?

MARTYR: Sure. But that kind of thinking implies that there's no grey area separating the two, which there is. There's a huge difference between something meant to disturb and unnerve as opposed to something that's intended to scare you.

AMBROSE: I think they're the same thing.

MARTYR: They're not. Something that's scary is intended to cause fear, to frighten you. However, something that's disturbing is intended to cause anxiety and be worrying.

AMBROSE: Seems like a synonym for one another. I guess it depends on the person on the receiving end of the story.

MARTYR: Yes?

AMBROSE: Like you and me, for instance. What do we do? We kill people—especially young men who prefer the company of other men.

MARTYR: *We* don't. *I* do.

AMBROSE: For some, the thought of that might be frightening, might give them dread. But it could also disturb them.

MARTYR: Can I finish my story?

AMBROSE: Please.

MARTYR: So, the guy takes the seventeen-year-old into the basement—

AMBROSE: I thought she was nineteen or twenty.

MARTYR: I said seventeen.

AMBROSE: You didn't. You said nineteen or twenty.

MARTYR: Does it matter?

AMBROSE: If she was underage, yes. It completely alters the dynamic of the story. Not to mention, it turns the story on its head—once frightening, now disturbing.

MARTYR: So, you agree there is a difference?

AMBROSE: Only in the sense that the dynamics of the story completely change when the girl is defined as under-age. It's unsavory. Grotesque.

MARTYR: Isn't that what true horror is?

AMBROSE: I thought this wasn't a horror story.

MARTYR: Can I finish?

AMBROSE: Yes.

MARTYR: So, he takes the girl—whatever age she was—into the cellar and shows her his prized possession: a small chamber made of concrete with a mechanical door that fastens shut and locks. There's nothing inside the room except for a computer, a small mattress, and a place where one might be able to relieve themselves. He tells her that he'll supply her with all the heroin she could ask for, all the prescription pills she could savor—the alprazolam, the diazepam, the flurazepam. Any "pam" you could think of—he'd make sure she'd have it. The only catch was she had to stay in the concrete tomb and never leave. In return, he would take care of her—provide her clothing, feed her, empty her waste bin. She would be his responsibility. So, what do you think she did? She agreed. The seventeen-year-old or nineteen-year-old or whatever age she was agreed to be taken care of and never leave the concrete box he had made for her. Apparently, she's still content with her decision. All the pills she can stomach, fresh clothing every morning, food whenever she rings for it. She lurks on certain chat forums—places on the internet better left undisturbed. They call her "Tomb Girl" and she's their sovereign.

AMBROSE: What's the point of that story?

MARTYR: Point?

AMBROSE: There has to be a point. A moral. A message. Something I missed.

MARTYR: It's whatever you make of it. She's a young woman with her whole life ahead of her who would rather willingly sit inside a concrete box and scroll on the internet all day—high out of her mind.

AMBROSE: It's a terrible story. There's no point to it other than to disturb the listener.

MARTYR: Sometimes that *is* the point.

AMBROSE: It reminds me of a far superior story. I can't remember the title, but it's about a young girl that's kept inside a cellar with a small window that looks out onto a busy street. Everyday people stop by the window and look down at the poor girl in her squalid little room—a grisly reminder than things can always be far worse. That's the point of the story.

MARTYR: Sometimes things don't have to be so didactic. A story can just be a story.

AMBROSE: Sounds like a plagiarized account of a better story.

MARTYR: Plagiarism implies that there's such a thing as originality.

AMBROSE: You don't believe plagiarism exists?

MARTYR: I don't believe in originality. Take for example, our art form—the slaughtering of precious young men with their future spread out in front of them. There's nothing original about the way in which I dispatch them. If this were a story, it would be mundane—trite at best.

AMBROSE: But there's such a thing as plagiarism.

MARTYR: It's just a construct invented by academia. It has no bearing in the real world.

AMBROSE: Unless you're a writer.

MARTYR: What's that supposed to mean?

AMBROSE: Just that it's—something most writers would fear. To be accused of plagiarism, I mean.

MARTYR: Masters of every craft bite off the talent of those that came before them. It's perfectly natural. I expect the authorities have noted my preference for the romanticism movement in art with each of my offerings being elaborately staged like a grotesque painting. The last one I did —that poor boy from Chelsea—I had arranged him like the ravished woman draped across the divan in Henry Fuseli's *The Nightmare*[2]. Now, is that plagiarism?

AMBROSE: More of an homage. A tribute. But that's an obscure reference. I doubt some authorities would even know who Fuseli was.

MARTYR: I could have easily arranged it so that it was similar to *La Grande Odalisque*[3]. Anything by Jean-Auguste-Dominique Ingres is a crowd pleaser.

AMBROSE: But far too obtuse. Besides, you would have had to wrap his head in a turban and locate a hookah to rest at his feet.

MARTYR: So, when does it become a direct copy?

AMBROSE: I guess if you had painted something—something that was a clear reference, a distinct lookalike to that particular painting.

MARTYR: So, you're saying plagiarism can only exist if it's the same art form? Writing vs. writing. Painting vs. painting. There's no such thing as a murder scene plagiarizing a painting.

AMBROSE: I think the ramifications for that would be far worse than mere plagiarism.

MARTYR: I take from things all around me all the time. I take and I take and I take. I never seem to give. I'm just not that way. Ambrose is, however. He's a giver. Always has been. Always will be. I have to think of the perfect painting to pair his death with—something grand in design, but tasteful in execution. Something that will make people marvel at his demise and think to themselves, "What a beautiful young man. What a glorious way for things to end."

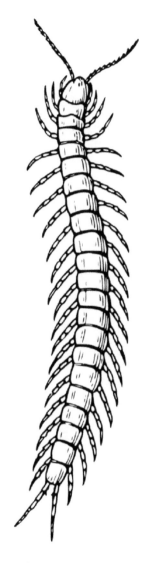

You've lost a lot of blood . . .

THE INVENTION OF SKIN

I often think of the first
creature to be given skin
and what it must have
felt like for them—
to be covered, to be
protected, to feel safe.
I often think of the first
wound blooming from
their precious skin and
how slowly it must have
healed, a scab to be worshiped
by zealots dressed in
expensive black hats.
I wonder how exquisite
it might feel to unspool
their skin like cheesecloth
until their body
was a murmur that could
no longer share their
most shameful secrets.
To hold their coat of flesh
in my arms like a broken child—
like a beggar sent to be
tortured until they weep.

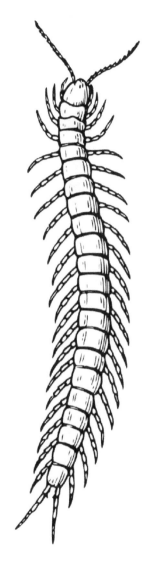

You've lost a lot of blood . . .

YOU'VE LOST A LOT OF BLOOD:
PART FOUR

[The following text includes the next four chapters of a novella,
You've Lost a Lot of Blood, *that Martyr Black had published by*
Carter Hill Press *in October of 2018.]*

PRESLEY

CHAPTER NINE

A police cruiser idles on the dirt driveway in front of the building, flashing red and blue lights.

Nadia crouches, shivering, beside the warehouse. Dani tends to her as an Officer wraps a blanket around her shoulders. Nadia wipes the oil from her face with a rag.

Tamsen leans against the car. Arms folded. Her eyes glazed over and distant as if still in shock.

She straightens, noticing the Sergeant exiting the warehouse and approaching the car. She's short, overweight. Her spiked hair—embellished with frosted tips.

The Sergeant pulls a walkie-talkie strapped to her shoulder against her mouth, mumbling.

Tamsen's eyes beg her for an answer, hopeful. "Anything–?"

The Sergeant shakes her head.

"What—happens now?" Tamsen asks.

"We'll file another report," the Sergeant explains. "Go from there."

Tamsen pauses, bewildered by the word: "Another–?"

"If he turns up, give the station a call. You still have the number–?" the Sergeant asks, brushing past Tamsen as she opens the car door.

"No. Uhh—I—Do you need his picture?"

"Already have it on file," the Sergeant says.

Tamsen squints, unsure. "You already... How–?"

"The report you filed last week."

Tamsen shakes her head. "Last week–? I—think you're mistaken."

"I wasn't here. But I have a copy of it. Chief recognized the address when we got the call."

"That's impossible," Tamsen says, frowning. "I never— we weren't here last week..."

The Sergeant grabs a folder on the front seat. Leafs through it until her fingers land on a page. "Presley Merrick Deerling. Date of birth: July 6. Weight: 82 pounds. Height–"

"Can I see that–?"

Tamsen reaches for the folder, but the Sergeant swipes it away. She grimaces, annoyed.

"You said it was a false alarm. A prank," the Sergeant says.

"No. That's not possible..."

"This picture was attached to the file–"

The Sergeant flashes a polaroid at her.

Tamsen pulls it close, her mouth hanging open in disbelief. The picture—Presley, smiling, in the familiar-looking backseat of Tamsen's car. The very same photo he had taken earlier.

"This—can't be," Tamsen says.

The Sergeant snatches the polaroid from her hands. "We'll send you another copy of the report."

The Sergeant whistles, hailing her partner. As she turns,

Tamsen notices the veins in the Sergeant's throat. Something thick and rope-like stretches beneath her skin.

She does a double take, squinting.

The Sergeant climbs into the car. Slams the door shut.

Tamsen taps on the window with trembling fingers.

The Sergeant lowers the window, annoyed.

"What if—we can't find him?" Tamsen asks.

"You'll find him," the Sergeant says, her eyes narrowing at Tamsen and her voice hardening. "We're stuck here until he sets us free."

Tamsen's mouth hangs open, trying to understand.

The Sergeant pushes a button, the window rising.

Peeling away from the building, the police cruiser soars down the dirt pathway and vanishes into the woods.

Tamsen swats the dust from the air, coughing.

Dani approaches her.

"What did they say–?" Dani asks.

"They said–"

But Tamsen stops herself. She bites her lip until it turns purple.

"– to let them know if anything changes."

Tamsen approaches Nadia beside the building. Dani follows.

"I'll keep looking for him," Dani says.

Tamsen helps Nadia off the ground, draping the weak woman's arm over her shoulder.

"Stay with me–?" Tamsen asks.

Nadia merely nods, leaning against her.

Tamsen stands in the frame of the carriage house's front door, eyes scanning the distant forest for any sign of Presley.

She folds her arms, bracing herself, as rain-soaked wind whips through the door and beats against her.

Nadia creeps down the stairs, wrapped in a bath robe. She squeezes her wet hair with a towel.

"Nothing–?" Nadia asks.

Tamsen grabs her raincoat. "I'm going back out."

Just then, Dani rips herself out of the darkness beyond where the house lights reach and races up the front steps into the house. She lowers her hood, wiping her rain-smeared face.

Tamsen eyes her, hopeful.

She hesitates. Shakes her head, mournful.

Tamsen deflates.

"We'll find him," Dani assures her.

"It's been four hours," Tamsen says, pacing the entry-way. "I—have to do something. I can't just—sit here. He could be scared. What if he's hurt–?"

Nadia staggers forward, color draining from her face.

"He'll be even more scared if he can't find you," she says.

She sways. Covers her mouth. Then, vomits into a nearby trashcan.

Tamsen wraps her arm around her, guiding her toward the couch. They sit, Nadia curling her head between her knees.

"Should we take her to the hospital?" Dani asks.

Tamsen looks panicked at the suggestion.

"I'm fine," Nadia says. "Please."

Tamsen rubs her shoulders gently. "She'll stay with me tonight."

"I'll go back out and look for him again before it gets dark," Dani says.

Tamsen softens, smiling at her—a wordless "thank you."

Dani nods, accepting her soundless gratitude. Then, heads back out the door and across the lawn toward the forest.

Tamsen's eyes follow Dani until she vanishes into the woods.

Nadia stirs on the couch, rubbing her head in visible agony. Tamsen notices. Drags the vomit-filled trashcan toward her.

"Again?" Tamsen asks.

"Headache," Nadia says.

"Something to eat–?"

Tamsen picks up the silver platter. Hesitates. Then, slams it back down on the credenza. She sits beside Nadia, nervously rubbing her fingers through her hair.

Nadia's eyes avoid Tamsen.

"What happened in there–?" Tamsen asks.

Nadia shakes her head, searching her thoughts. She looks at Tamsen, eyes filled with fear. "I—can't... I don't remember..."

Tamsen turns away. Looks out the rain-washed window.

"I'm—sorry," Nadia whispers.

Tamsen doesn't respond.

She looks at the main house in the distance—a fortress tethered against the storm-swept horizon. It's then she notices a dark shape watching her from the attic window.

LATER THAT NIGHT, TAMSEN STAYS UP AND WATCHES THE RAIN BEAT hard against the windows. Lightning flickers, a dark silhouette appearing between the colonnade of oak at the forest's edge. She squints, rubbing her eyes, as the figure approaches.

Another flash of lightning to reveal—it's Presley.

Drenched in glistening black oil, he staggers into the clearing and limps toward the carriage house. He winces, rain battering him and slowing him as he hobbles through the monsoon.

A gust of wind shoots across his path, leveling him.

On hands and knees, he drags himself toward the front steps. Ribbons of oil swirl down his body, vanishing as the rain pummels him.

Tamsen dashes outside, switching on the porch lights, and covers her mouth when she sees him in all his monstrous glory.

"Pres," she cries out.

Darting down the steps and across the lawn, Tamsen holds Presley in her arms.

His eyelids flutter open for a moment. Lips open to speak but can only murmur. Eyelids close again.

Tamsen pulls him tight against her. Shovels him from the ground and carries his body toward the house.

"Nadia," she calls out.

Limping up the steps as she cradles Presley in her arms, Tamsen disappears inside the small house.

NADIA, ARMS FILLED WITH BLANKETS AND A FIRST AID KIT, approaches the bathroom. The faint clatter of feet approaching behind the door.

The door opens, Tamsen appearing in the frame.

Nadia peers inside.

Sees Presley—dripping wet—standing by the window.

Suddenly, his eyes snap to her.

She recoils.

Tamsen tiptoes into the hall, closing the door behind her.

"How is he?" Nadia asks, passing the blankets and emergency kit to Tamsen.

"He's not hurt. Thankfully," Tamsen says. "Needs a bath though."

"I'll get it ready," Nadia says.

"You've done enough."

"I don't mind."

Tamsen squeezes Nadia's hand with a silent "thank you." Then, turns the door handle. Slips back inside the room.

———

LATER, AFTER TAMSEN HAD DRAWN HIS BATH AND LET HIM SOAK for a while, she slips back into the bathroom and finds her little brother lounging in the bathroom's clawfoot bathtub. Wisps of steam rise from the scalding hot bath water.

Presley drags a washcloth along his oil-soaked arms. Squeezing it in his fists, black sludge hoses the water.

He stirs, uncomfortable, as soon as she enters. Tamsen averts her eyes.

"I won't look. I promise," she says.

She grabs the trashcan beside the toilet. Sets it down near the bathtub.

"In case you need it again."

Glances at Presley for a reaction. Nothing.

She paces beside him. Unsure what to say.

"How do you feel–?"

"My head hurts," he says quietly.

Tamsen softens.

"Where were you–? What happened?" she asks.

Presley doesn't answer.

He stares at the dark bath water, unblinking.

Tamsen notices a pile of his wet clothing discarded on the floor. She scoops it up.

Tamsen turns away, dumping Presley's clothing in the marble sink. She braces herself against the counter, eyes avoiding her reflection in the mirror.

"I—thought I lost you," she says.

Then, Tamsen pivots, facing him.

He winces. Covers himself.

"I'm sorry I'm not better at this," she says.

Tamsen inches toward the bathtub, cautious.

"Clean slate–?"

But Presley doesn't react.

Tamsen shrinks, deflating. Lowers her head.

"I'll be outside when you're finished," she says. "Call if you need anything."

Tamsen shuffles toward the door. Glancing back to Presley one final time. He looks away.

She shuts the door, disappearing, and doesn't seem to notice the wire slithering beneath the skin of her brother's shoulder.

CHAPTER TEN

Tamsen's eyelids flutter open.

A grey sky threatening with more rain framed in the window above her bed.

She rolls over on her side, greeted by Presley. Dressed in pajamas, he stands beside her bed. His lips crease with a smile. The cheerful face she's always known.

"Hey," she says.

Tamsen pushes herself up, leaning against the headboard.

"Everything alright?"

Presley nods. "Fine."

Tamsen rubs her eyes, yawning. "You're sure?"

She presses her hand against his forehead, feeling his temperature. Checks his hands and arms for bruises.

"Nadia says if I help her with chores today, she'll show me the library," he says. "Twelve-hundred first editions."

"So. We'll stay–?"

"Why wouldn't we?"

Presley crawls off the bed, moving out of the room.

Tamsen stirs in bed, unsure.

She looks up and notices a black centipede peering down at her from the edge of the ceiling fan.

———

Tamsen runs a pot under the faucet, the phone pressed against her ear.

"Hi. Yes, I filed a report yesterday and I'd like to withdraw it," she says.

"What's your name?" the Officer on the other end of the line asks her.

Tamsen sets the pot on the stove, cranking up the gas. "Last name, Deerling. First name, Tamsen."

"For a missing person?" the Officer asks.

"Yes," Tamsen says. "My brother. It was a mistake. I'm sorry to–"

Tamsen winces, the phone releasing a shrill, metal pulse.

The Officer's voice cuts out.

Tamsen checks the phone. Then, pushes it against her ear.

"What was–?"

"It's going to start all over again," a voice whispers to her.

The line goes quiet. Tamsen holds the phone closer.

A livid screech. Metal against metal.

Tamsen jumps. She hangs up the phone.

———

Tamsen's face—washed in a silver glow as she sits in front of the computer. Hands guiding the mouse with nervous precision, her eyes remain fixed on her work.

On the computer screen, a grotesque face stares back at her, confined to a small window inside a design program. The creature's leathery skin as transparent as amber and shrouded with a curtain of cobwebs. The crown of its bulbous head—eaten away and exposing long, thin spindles of insect legs.

She drags the cursor over one of the limbs fanning out from the creature's cracked skull, adding definition to the artwork with an animated paintbrush.

Clicks "File: Save As."

Types in "You've_Lost_a_Lot_of_Blood_Design_1A."

Presses down on the mouse. Saved.

She stiffens in her seat, sensing something watching her.

Turning, her eyes dart to the metal sculpture looming in the corner. She scans the golden plaque. "ENGINE."

Eyes returning to the screen, she opens a file titled, "You've Lost a Lot of Blood Prototype."

On the screen, a small map of the game's industrial-style setting framed beside a text window filled with the game's coding.

Tamsen scans each line of text, her eyes widening.

She clicks "File: Print."

TAMSEN TIPTOES DOWN THE HALLWAY, CLUTCHING SHEETS OF paper. She slows as she nears the attic stairwell, the sounds of a woman's sobs becoming louder.

Reaching the foot of the stairs, she peers up at the landing outside the attic suite.

Inching up the stairs, she reaches the door. The sobbing grows deafening.

Tamsen reaches out. Hesitates. Then, knocks. "Ms. Zimpago–?"

Finally, a break in the sobbing. Muffled whimpers.

Tamsen waits. There's no response.

"Ms. Zimpago, are you alright–?"

She waits again. Finally, Iris' soft, birdlike voice responds from the other side of the door.

"What do you want–?"

Tamsen swallows, eyes going over the pages in her hands. "I was—going over some of the coding for the game to run a demo of my design..."

She pauses, waiting for Iris to respond. Nothing.

"I found something. It's a large break in the coding. It looks like it was designed by Mr. Zimpago to be part of the player's experience."

Tamsen's eyes wander to the statue of the Engineer beside the door. A wide mouth made of iron grins at her.

"The program is locked so the user can only access the system once. But, theoretically, they could manipulate the code break and use it to play the game again. It would be like creating a new gaming account. A new version of themselves."

Once again, no response. Tamsen presses her ear against the door, listening.

"Ms. Zimpago–?"

The crash of glass shattering.

"GO AWAY!"

Tamsen lurches away from the door, flying down the stairs.

Glancing back at the attic door, she hastens down the hall until the sounds of Iris' sobs are dimmed to murmurs.

Her pace slows as she reaches Abbas Zimpago's bedroom door.

Peering through the window fixed at the center of his door, she regards her employer's motionless body. She scans his linen-wrapped face, glistening black goggles staring back at her.

Pressing against the frame, her hand leans into the scanner beside the door. It chirps. The screen burns bright green.

ACCESS GRANTED.

She pulls her hand away, dismayed.

The bolt retracts with a thud. The door swings open.

Puzzled, Tamsen remains without movement. Mouth opens, eyes searching for an explanation.

Bathed in a pale white glow, the room more closely resembles the sterility of an ICU.

The dim pulse of the machines monitoring his vitals fill the space with a steady hum.

Tamsen approaches the bed, eyes scanning the sparsely decorated room.

Towering over his small body, her eyes drift from his bandaged feet to his linen-wrapped face.

She notices a black spot blooming beneath the edge of his pillow. Presses her finger against it. Still damp.

Rubs her fingers together. Slick like oil.

She reaches out, about to remove his goggles when her eyes snap to the floor:

An origami swan. Discarded beneath the bed.

Tamsen bends down. Picks it up.

Covers her mouth in horror as she realizes—it's Presley's.

Tamsen tucks the swan in her pocket and darts out of the room. Slams the door shut as she scurries down the hall and toward the conservatory where she finds Presley and Nadia enjoying their afternoon tea.

Tamsen tucks the swan behind her back as she approaches them.

"He recited the entire plot of *Wuthering Heights* to me until I showed him the library," Nadia says, chuckling.

Immediately Nadia seems to notice Tamsen's flushed face.

"Everything alright, dear–?"

Tamsen catches her breath. "Yes. I—uhm—just need…"

She turns, motioning for Nadia to follow.

Nadia searches Presley for a reaction, smiling, as she moves away from the table. He doesn't even notice her absence, eyes glued to the book.

Tamsen leads Nadia further down the path until they're out of his earshot.

She reveals the small white swan. "I found this. You remember–?"

Nadia nods. "Presley made–"

"It was in Mr. Zimpago's room."

Tamsen passes the folded paper to Nadia.

"You went in?" Nadia asks, bewildered.

"Do you know how it got there?"

Nadia holds the swan close to her face, mouth hanging open. "I—couldn't even guess."

"Mr. Zimpago. He can't—move, can he?" Tamsen asks.

Nadia hesitates to answer, seemingly puzzled by the question.

"I—don't know what to think," Tamsen says. "There's a reason it was in there.

Glancing at Presley, she crushes the paper swan in her fist.

CHAPTER ELEVEN

Presley climbs into bed, dragging sheets over him. Tamsen sits at the end of his bed. She eyes the hardcover book on his nightstand. "I—can read to you–? If you want."

"You don't want to," Presley says.

Tamsen shrinks, hurt. He's right.

"I wouldn't offer if I didn't–"

But she knows he's not convinced. She watches him as he rolls over on his side, facing away from the light.

"I'm almost finished with it anyway," he says.

Tamsen lifts herself off the bed and reaches for the lamp. She pauses, softening, as she looks at her brother. Mouth hangs open for a moment with muted words. Finally, they come out:

"Pres. Just because—we don't like the same things... It —doesn't mean I don't love you."

Presley turns, light washing half of his face.

Tamsen searches his face. She notices a small bump below his eyelid. It's pointed, sharp-looking.

He stares at his sister, puzzled. "Tam–?"

She pushes her finger against it. Lurches back as it stirs beneath his skin gently.

Presley winces at her touch.

"There's—something..."

She grabs the lamp, holding it against his face.

He covers his eyes, squirming.

"What are you doing?" he asks her.

Tamsen guides the light across his skin until she realizes the bump has vanished.

She lowers her aim, setting the lamp down.

Just then, a knock at the front door.

Tamsen opens the front door. Dani, dressed in a damp raincoat, appears in the frame. She holds the blowtorch.

"Finishing up," she says. "Just wanted to see if there's anything I could do–"

Tamsen drops her shoulders, deflating.

"We're getting by," she says, moving into the living room.

Dani, confused, follows. She sets the torch beside the door.

"I just—wanted to see if he needed anything."

Tamsen folds her arms. Swallows hard.

"He's fine."

Dani looks at her skeptically.

"I just thought–"

She stops, recognizing she won't give in.

"If he needs anything. I'm around."

Dani starts to leave.

Tamsen hesitates.

"I think..."

She stops, searching for the words.

"Something happened to him when he went into the game," she says. "He's—different."

"How–?"

Tamsen shakes her head. "I don't know. It's like he's—changing. Except he still hates me."

She sits on the couch, wiping tears from her eyes.

"He doesn't hate you," Dani assures her.

"He should."

Tamsen exhales, shoulders drooping as if her body were buckling under the pressure of the secret.

"I blame him for what happened to our parents," she says quietly. "I can't look at him without being reminded of it. I thought of all the different ways I could leave him. Like he was a dog. Couple months ago. I took him to help me do some laundry. Gave him a dollar to go to the vending machine. And when he wasn't looking—I got back in my car. Drove away."

She covers her mouth at the memory.

"I drove around for a few hours. Realized what I had done and finally went back. Police were already there. I told them it was an accident. That I didn't mean to."

Tamsen looks away from Dani. She sobs.

"I'm a monster. I'd do everything different if I could."

Dani hesitates. She wraps an arm around her. Tamsen settles into her embrace, crying. She pulls her closer.

"You went back for him," Dani says. "That was your second chance."

Tamsen pulls away from her. Confused.

"Why are you being so nice to me?"

Dani smiles. "Think of it as a clean slate."

Their eyes fasten to one another, an invisible electrical current pulling their bodies closer together.

Tamsen presses her lips against Dani's. Then, pulls away. Her face flushes, as if humiliated.

Dani grabs her, their mouths pushing together.

Tamsen pants, Dani gliding her tongue up her neck and circling the rim of her ear.

Tamsen unbuttons her pants, kicking them off as they corkscrew around her ankles. With their mouths glued together, Dani rips off Tamsen's underwear.

She kneels. Buries her face where Tamsen's legs meet, devouring her.

Tamsen rakes her head back, moaning with pleasure.

Her hands search her, rubbing her stomach and massaging her breasts as her legs spread further.

Tamsen hears the chirp of metal scraping against metal.

She lifts her head slightly, something catching her attention in the floor-length mirror across the room.

Her eyes lower to below her waist where Dani's reflection should be. Instead, the wrought iron creature. A wire-veined framework. It shoves its head between her thighs, wires zigzagging across her skin and about to coil inside her when –

Tamsen screams, jumping up.

Dani lurches back, wiping threads of spit from her mouth.

"Get out," Tamsen cries.

Dani flinches, horrified and confused.

"GET THE FUCK OUT!"

Dani swipes her raincoat. Dashes out the door.

Tamsen follows close behind, bolting it shut. She chokes on short, shallow gasps.

She leans against the frame and lowers herself until she's slumped on the floor. Holds her knees tight against her chest, sobbing, and remains there until daylight.

CHAPTER TWELVE

Tamsen leans against the desk, resting her hand against her face as she stares at the computer screen in Zimpago's office.

She nurses a glass of whiskey. Pours more from the bottle.

On the screen, the "Spider Head" creature glares at her.

She clicks "File: Move to Trash."

The grotesque face—sucked from the screen, vanishing.

Tamsen rubs her head, exhausted. Dragging herself out of her seat, she moves to the windows overlooking the garden.

She notices Dani kneeling beside a carpet of purple milkweed with a pair of pruning shears. She rises, wiping the sweat from her forehead.

She looks up at the window, her eyes meeting Tamsen's.

Tamsen stiffens, skittish. Remains unmoving. Caught.

Dani flashes her middle finger. Then, collects the nearby wheelbarrow and moves away from the house.

Deflated, Tamsen returns to the computer.

Slumps in her chair.

Tamsen reaches for the mouse, her hand knocking it on the floor. Bending over, she peers under the desk and notices a USB device hiding behind one of the legs.

She pulls it out. Studies the writing written on the band of packing tape—Zimpago interview unreleased.

Tamsen inserts the device into the monitor. She waits.

On the screen, a black window pops up. An animated hourglass appears, the video loading.

Tamsen clicks, the dark window filling the entire screen. She presses "Play."

On the screen, a wrinkled, sun-wizened face fills the frame—Abbas Zimpago. Outfitted in expensive black, his tailored suit accents the thinness of his frame as gold bracelets dangle from his toothpick wrists.

An off-camera Interviewer questions him.

"We received a lot of fan requests to ask you about *You've Lost a Lot of Blood*," the Interviewer explains. "Is there anything you can tell us–?"

Zimpago grins, as if pleased to be asked. His lips wrinkle. "*Sono desiderosi*. It's about—*la trasformazione*. The best games are like viruses you can't cure. They change us. Stay with us long after we've finished playing. *You've Lost a Lot of Blood* will be an experience like no other."

Tamsen, her face washed in silver, stares at the screen. Light flickers across her eyes as the video plays.

"Some people have taken to social media to announce their plans to boycott the release," the Interviewer says. "Can you explain why the user can only play the game once?"

Zimpago stirs in his seat, adjusting his ascot. "If we want virtual reality to be as life-like as possible, do we receive second chances in life? I appreciate the dedication of my fans. But this project was made so that my creation could touch as many people as possible. It's my gift to the world."

"You said in an interview recently that your new game, *You've Lost a Lot of Blood*, is intended only for users between the age of ten and twenty. Why is that?" the Interviewer asks.

"*L'immaginazione* of the youth is the most sacred thing in the world," Zimpago says.

"What do you have to say in response to the allegations made about the violence in your games by concerned parents? Especially the Challis Family–? As you know, their daughter won the–"

Just then, Zimpago's faceless, well-dressed Handler enters the frame and blocks Zimpago from the camera.

"Mr. Zimpago has no comment," the handler says. "We're done here."

The video cuts to black.

Tamsen moves the cursor over the "Internet" icon. Clicks.

Her fingers flick across the keyboard. Types in: "Zimpago Challis."

The first result: a link to an obituary—"Dani Challis."

She clicks on the link. Eyes scan the web page.

Tamsen covers her mouth, in horror.

It's a picture of Dani.

She looks closer. Sees a silver earring in the shape of a snake coiling around the rim of her ear.

She reads the article: *"Dani Challis died on Tuesday, March 12th at the age of 20 as the result of a brain aneurysm. Dani was a student at the University of New Hampshire. While in school, she served as the President of the Gaming League. She had recently won a gaming contest sponsored by the internationally acclaimed Zimpago Project."*

Tamsen clicks "File: Print." The machine hums, printing.

She finds another article: "Challis Family blame daughter's unexpected death on violent video games."

She presses on the link. A picture of Abbas Zimpago greets her.

Tamsen reads further down the page.

The article reads: "She wasn't my daughter anymore," Laura Challis, Dani's mother, told sources. "The games had changed her." Her daughter, an avid game enthusiast, had won an exclusive all-access pass to new gaming technology at Mr. Zimpago's private estate the month prior to her death.

Tamsen's eyes widen further as she reads. Reaches for the mouse. Clicks "Print."

She knocks over a miniature statue on the desk. The figurine shatters on the floor.

Kneeling, she swipes at the bits wedged beneath the desk's leg. Hands fumbling with one of the desk drawers for support, she presses against a gilded handle.

A panel in the wall slides open.

Tamsen looks up, startled. Approaches the opening, a passageway stretches in front of her.

She disappears inside.

Every inch of the low-ceiling vault—the glistening reflective surfaces of dark metal.

The dim murmuring of whispers.

Tamsen approaches a candlelit altar built from steel.

The mirror-like walls—an ornate mosaic of various parts of human anatomy threaded with centipede-like wires and cables. Some extremities are attached to cranks and gears.

Faces are lost in a labyrinth of couplings and spindles as long and thin as insect legs.

Tamsen winces. Gnarled mouths scowl at her as she passes.

Peering inside the small metal bowl fixed at the center of the altar, she covers her mouth at the sight -

Presley's polaroid camera. Her cellphone.

She snatches them from the bowl. Then, notices something remaining—a silver earring in the shape of a snake.

She shoves the earring in her pocket and tears out of the room.

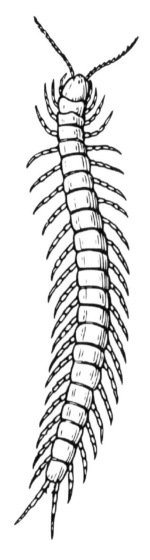

You've lost a lot of blood . . .

BODIES MADE OF HONEYCOMB: December 7th, 2018

Long before I had met Ambrose, I became involved with a young man who had a distinct and somewhat unnerving predilection. He was boyishly handsome in his looks—the kind of youthful vitality that could not be persuaded to temper its enthusiasm. He had a way of speaking, a way of commanding the room and others around him as if they were mere servants to his fancy. I often found myself to be completely enraptured by his charm, his good graces, and his exceptional table manners at the finest eating establishments in the city.

Our lovemaking sessions were robust and vigorous to say the least. Though I'm typically opposed to having another man's genitals smashing into my colon despite what many other gay men describe as a heavenly feeling unlike any other, I was entirely submissive with him and eager to receive him at any time and any place. Even in public sometimes if we were able to find a secluded location in a neighborhood park or a parking garage.

Although our lovemaking eventually tired and became tedious fumbles that even teenage lovers might find awkward and appalling, I can assure you that I did not kill him because he grew fatigued of my sexual appetite in the sack. I didn't kill him because he overdressed at parties or adored any opportunity to show himself off as the superior in thought and personality despite my obvious grooming as a prime bachelor from one of the state's most noble families. I killed him because he shared with me something so abhorrent that my ear could scarcely credit his words.

Every Sunday, he would visit a nearby hospital and claim to be a guest of a patient in the ward where most of the patients undergoing chemotherapy are warehoused.

This was his *"peccadillo,"* as he lovingly referred to it. Always eager to share his flair for other languages. When admitted by a nurse, he would stalk the hallways in the ward and look for a room where a patient was sleeping. Whether it was the halo of light that glinted from their bald head or the tubes securing their nose, he couldn't be certain what attracted him to these poor, hopeless souls. Regardless, he was all too eager to enjoy himself while he was there.

Unzipping his pants and pulling out his manhood, he stroked himself until he came—watching them as they dozed, probably high on morphine. It didn't matter to him if it was a man or a woman or even a child. To him, their bodies were exotic gardens blooming with disease. To him, they were hardly human—bodies made of honeycomb instead. He said he felt no pity for them, felt nothing remotely like sin or perversion when he contemplated the seriousness of what he was actually doing.

There was no remorse, no semblance of sympathy, no hint of compassion.

I regretted how I had so unabashedly given myself to him—my body, my mind. I felt ill, as if my intestines were curling and turning black from when he had last sprayed my insides during one of our more passionate rendezvous. I felt as if I had been polluted—as if my body no longer belonged to me, as if there were a giant black tapeworm coiling itself inside me and growing more and more every time I thought of him and his penchant for marking their poor, defenseless bodies with himself—the pleasure he took from wiping himself on their bald heads.

So, I decided to kill him.

I called him over one night and arranged the bed so that he thought we wouldn't be talking much. When he was finally naked and preparing himself for the main event, I took an empty champagne bottle and smashed it over his head. I smashed him again and again, the bottle cracking apart and the bits sparkling on the floor like bits of sea glass. I twisted the broken pieces into his face until I saw a white fang of bone poking through his skin. When I was certain he was dead, I shaved him until he was completely bald. He resembled one of those monks from the 15th or 16th centuries—a pastiche of a Holy man when I knew full well there was nothing holy or sacred about him.

After I had shaved his head and dressed again in his clothing, I drove his lifeless body out to the old rock quarry just outside of town and left him there to be found in the morning by workers. I couldn't help but laugh, thinking how he resembled the kinds of people he had manipulated and used for his own satisfaction. There was something so satisfying about seeing him lie there—splayed out against the rocks, arms raised above his head as if questioning God why he had been taken at such a young age. He almost resembled Sir John Everett Millais' exquisite painting of *Ophelia*[1]. Rain began to sprinkle as he laid there like a Danish princess, rainwater threatening to drown him just as she had been drowned in the river.

I wondered if I was right to kill him—if I had saved some poor innocent child from his cruelty, or if I was no better than him: a monster capable of performing the most sadistic and vicious acts. Surely there must be something said for my intentions, my yearning to smear him from the world and others like him.

Then again, it begs the question: why do I kill? What satisfaction do I derive from taking the life from someone as if I were squeezing the juice from a lemon? Am I a monster because I killed him? Of course, he deserved to die.

But then, do I for what I've done?

Am I no better than him?

Does morality serve a purpose here, and if so, who comes out on top? Or are we both monsters that deserve no sympathy?

Not long after I killed him, I had learned that there were others like him—others that unabashedly delighted in the thought of the young and old afflicted with terminal illness and undergoing chemotherapy. They called themselves "The Wax Priests"—a carefully selected and highly exclusive group of men of all ages with a certain penchant for disease.

I didn't know how I might set about my plans, but I knew for certain I wanted to find each of them and make them suffer.

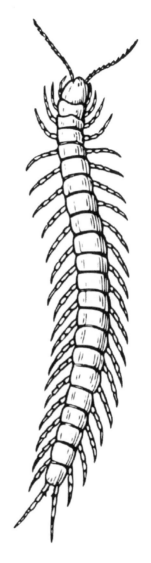

You've lost a lot of blood . . .

DIASPORA

I watch them from my window
Little priests made from wax
Their melted faces
Their bodies made of honeycomb
They drip like burning candles
and walk as if they carry
the secret of a language
long since dead and
never to be resuscitated
Skin like Chantilly lace
Shiny like an alligator's hide
I watch them as they file up and down
the empty streets where they had died
Holy men left to rust in the morning sun

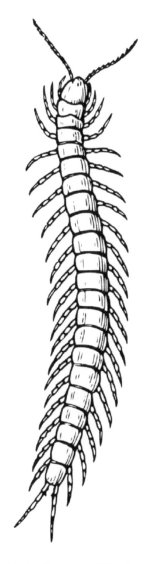

You've lost a lot of blood . . .

YOU'VE LOST A LOT OF BLOOD:

PART FIVE

[The following text includes the next two chapters of a novella, You've Lost a Lot of Blood, *that Martyr Black had published by Carter Hill Press in October of 2018.]*

CHAPTER THIRTEEN

Tamsen hastens out of the main house and makes her way toward the carriage house at the end of the causeway. She flies inside the small house, darts up the stairs, and sprints into Presley's bedroom.

He turns away, face pressed against the rain-hosed window.

"Where's Nadia?" Tamsen as Presley doesn't answer.

She hurls his suitcase on the bed. Flings open his closet. Grabs an armful of clothes. Dumps them in his suitcase.

Presley won't look at her, distracted by the rain.

"We're leaving," Tamsen says, zipping his suitcase shut.

"We can't," Presley says.

"In the car. Let's go."

She drags his suitcase into the hall, disappearing.

If she had stayed, she might have seen Presley twitch, a long thin shape stirring beneath his skin and coiling around his throat. She might have seen her brother wince in agony, metal spikes bursting across his face and braiding his head with thick cables of wires. Even worse, she might have seen him lift his head, revealing a sinewy vent of tissue fixed at the center of his throat. The flesh around the device—burned red as if cauterized.

Instead, Tamsen sees none of that.

She darts into her room and snatches clothing from the closet, pouring the heap into her suitcase. Zipping it shut, she hauls her suitcase off the bed and flies out of the room. She doesn't seem to notice the sweatshirt she's left dangling in the bedroom closet.

Tamsen hastens out of the house, dragging suitcases. She unlocks the trunk and loads the baggage.

Dragging the driver's door open, she slides into the seat. Pushes the key into the ignition. The car purrs alive.

She pants, out of breath.

Tamsen glances back at the house—the empty door frame filled with light. Presley's nowhere in sight.

"Pres," she calls out.

No response.

Climbing out of the car as it idles, she scales the front steps and flits back inside the house.

Tamsen rushes to the foot of the stairs, calling: "Pres, let's go!"

Presley doesn't answer.

Tamsen grips the bannister, about to dash up the stairs when:

She hears the chirp of metal dragging against metal. The sound—coming from upstairs.

She recoils, paling.

Looks around the room for a weapon. Spies the blowtorch Dani had left beside the front door.

Swiping it, she creeps up the stairs. Aims the weapon.

As she reaches the top of the stairs, she finds Presley's door open a sliver. The room—pitch black.

Pushing the door open with the blowtorch, Tamsen

peers into the dark room. Finds Presley standing beside the window, looking off.

Her hands fumble along the wall for the light switch. Flicks it up and down. No light.

Gripping the blowtorch tighter, she inches into the room.

"Pres–?"

Presley twitches when he speaks as if it pains him to talk. His voice—thin, as if his lungs were filled with iron.

"There's somebody outside," he says.

Tamsen shrinks at the unfamiliar sound of his voice. "What–?"

Presley turns, the light from the corridor washing his face. Tamsen covers her mouth at the sight.

Presley flinches, dagger-tipped metal wires blooming from his skin and snaking across his body.

His neck extends, gears made from muscle lining the wire-threaded shaft of his throat. His cheeks bulge with crankshaft mechanisms spiraling from underneath his skin.

He whimpers. Inches toward her.

"It—hurts," he says quietly.

With trembling hands, Tamsen aims the blowtorch at him.

"You're—not my brother," she says.

Presley groans, kneeling. Lowering his head, he reveals a wire-threaded pipe sprouting from the crown of his skull.

He rakes his head back in agony, his wrists snapping backward as pistons shoot through his arms. He screams, wires whipping inside his mouth as his jaws stretch further.

Wires burst from his mouth, skirting across the floor toward Tamsen.

She lurches back, stumbling out of the room and into the hallway.

Fishing in her pockets for the house key, she locks his bedroom door.

She jumps, screaming, as Presley's body slams against the door. The hiss of wires thrashing.

The door handle shakes, twisting.

"What did you do to my brother?" she asks.

Wires whip beneath the door, belting Tamsen.

"It's me, Tam," he shouts at her from beyond the door.

Tamsen shrinks until she's backed into a corner. The blowtorch–her only defense.

She hears the sound of the front door creaking open. Footsteps enter the house, creeping up the steps.

Body pressed against the wall, she sneaks down the corridor. Hiding, she aims the blowtorch at the stairwell.

Lightning flickers, throwing a dark shadow against the wall as the figure nears the top of the steps.

Tamsen swallows hard. Before another moment of hesitation.

She screams, vaulting around the corner. Pulls the handle. A stream of fire bursts from the nozzle, hosing Dani's face. The flames lick her head, revealing a set of steel wires beneath her skin. She widens her blackened jaw, releasing a guttural growl from her wire-clogged throat. Charging at Tamsen, she grabs her by the throat and squeezes. Then, pins her against the wall as she squirms helplessly.

"The game's not finished," Dani says.

Slamming her head against the wall, she knocks Tamsen to the ground. The blowtorch slips from Tamsen's hands and rolls across the hall.

She lunges for it as he grabs her legs.

Swiping the torch, Tamsen swivels and sprays Dani with the nozzle again.

More of her face blisters, revealing sheets of metal beneath.

"You're already dead," Tamsen shouts at her, slamming the blowtorch against Dani's head.

Dani's knees buckle, hands grasping at the air. She falls back, flying down the stairwell until she crashes against the floor.

Lightning flickers, her limp body flashing in the light as it lies crushed at the foot of the stairs.

Tamsen coughs. Steadies her breathing.

Inching down the steps, she approaches Dani's lifeless body.

Her open eyes—doll-like and vacant. Her face—charred black. The exposed pink tissue glinting with flecks of light.

"It's—a machine," Tamsen says quietly.

Wiping her mouth, her eyes snap to the top of the stairwell. Sees Presley standing there.

Pistons fire, pulverizing his head. Gears revolve, wrenching his flesh until his face is a sinewy mask of exposed muscle.

She jumps out of the way as he scampers down the stairs, vaulting over Dani's dead body.

Tamsen ducks, more wires flying at her as Presley passes. He darts out of the house, the vent in his throat releasing a deep growl. He dashes across the lawn and heads for the forest.

"What have you done to my brother?" she calls after him.

But he doesn't respond.

Tamsen tosses on her raincoat. Grabs a flashlight. Then, she darts out of the house, chasing after him deep into the forest.

PRESLEY RACES DOWN THE NARROW PATHWAY, LEAPING OVER fallen branches and dodging shrubs.

He grunts, wheels and cylinders cranking as they bury deeper in his skin. Black fluid drips, exploding from the wheezing steel pipe fixed in his head.

Tamsen's flashlight shimmers through the thicket. She bounds after him, racing toward the Silo.

"Where the fuck is he?" she shouts.

Glancing back and noticing Tamsen approaching, Presley hurries further away. Dodges between trees and meanders off the pathway.

He hurtles over a moss-covered log.

Tamsen scales the same log. Trips. Slams against the ground.

Presley gains the advantage, sprinting ahead.

Tamsen wipes herself clean. Gets back on her feet. Staggers after Presley.

Glancing back at her, Presley accelerates as if he were powered by a train engine. Grunting. Faster and faster.

He dashes out onto the ledge of a large rock. Looks back as he sails ahead. And falls –

Plummeting over the side of the ridge, he crashes against the riverbed.

Tamsen covers her mouth, screaming.

Presley—splayed, lying without movement. Blood as black as oil—smeared against the rocks.

Tamsen crawls the ledge, lowering herself to the ground. She circles his lifeless body, training the flashlight on him.

Presley's body twitches.

The steel pipe fountains like a geyser. Black sludge

hoses the ground. Tamsen shields her face, oil showering her.

A giant centipede—an engine—slithers out from the drooling hole in the imposter's head.

The insect's body—glistening black, smeared with fluids. Its chain of legs—iridescent metal.

The creature leaps across the riverbed. Slowing as it crawls further away from Presley's body, it's without movement.

Tamsen studies Presley's skinless face. Looks closer—his mouth gagged and overflowing with wires.

"You're not my brother," she says.

She steadies her shallow gasps until she grunts. Tightens her fingers around the flashlight with a threat.

CHAPTER FOURTEEN

Tamsen, face smeared with oil, darts out of the forest. She hastens into the clearing. Toward the carriage house.

Rain drizzles. A distant rumble of thunder.

Her car—still idling in the driveway.

She races up the front path. Stops. Finds Nadia standing in the open doorway.

Sees Dani's body where she had left it—crumpled in a heap at the foot of the stairs. Nadia can scarcely speak, her head shaking in disbelief.

"What did she–?"

Nadia's voice trails off, in shock.

Tamsen squints. Thinks she sees a strand of hair poking through Nadia's hijab. She looks closer. It's a wire.

Nadia shrinks, noticing Tamsen's fury as she approaches.

Tamsen lunges at Nadia, screaming.

Nadia dodges the attack, hurrying across the driveway and toward the main house in the distance.

Tamsen follows, close behind.

"What have you done to him?"

Her screams echo through the nearby pines.

───────

TAMSEN CHASES NADIA TO THE MAIN HOUSE. SHE DARTS INTO THE marble entryway. A predator on the hunt.

She notices the door leading to the Armory cracked open, light spilling into the foyer.

Crouching, she skulks toward the doorway.

Tamsen creeps into the room. It's empty.

She weaves between rows of glass cases filled with various weapons—the blades glinting at her in the light.

The ceiling camera rotates, following her as she moves.

Glancing back, she knocks against a glass case. Steadies her balance. Squints, peering inside—the tactical hammer axe.

Pulling down on the glass door's level, she reaches inside and grabs the weapon's handle. Holds the blade close to her face. Admires her reflection.

The scurrying of feet outside the door.

Head snaps up, ears perking at the noise of prey on the move. She grips the axe's handle tighter.

───────

TAMSEN ENTERS THE GRAND HALL, BRANDISHING THE AXE. A shimmering screen of water crashes into the room, mist rising in thick clouds from the foaming apron of water.

"You knew it the whole time," she says, circling the edge of the room. "You took us there on purpose."

Tamsen raises the blade above her shoulders, about to strike.

Thunder crashes.

The power goes out—light sucked from the room. The waterfall flickers out, vanishing.

Lightning flashes in the skylight, light drenching the room and revealing Nadia as she crouches on the floor.

Tamsen's eyes narrow at her. Slams the axe down. Crash.

Nadia screams, dodging the blow. Tears out of the room, sprinting into the Armory.

Nadia lunges for a glass case filled with a giant Medieval Mace. Tries to open the door. Won't budge. Locked.

Tamsen appears in the doorway, swinging the axe.

Releases a deafening battle cry.

Nadia swipes a dagger fastened to the wall and heads for the entryway.

Nadia races toward the door, Tamsen on her tail.

Clutching the knife, she fumbles with the handle. Ducks, screaming, as Tamsen hurls the axe at her.

The blade misses her head. Slams into the wall.

Nadia flings the door open. The dagger slips from her hands.

Nadia flies down the front steps, bolting toward her car. Pats her pockets. No keys. She pulls on the doors. Locked. The alarm rings—a deafening pulse.

Tamsen appears in the doorway, flying down the steps with the axe swinging in her arms.

Nadia screams, deserting her car and heading for the forest.

From a distance, Tamsen watches Nadia stumble

through the trees and dodge her flashlight. Kicking off her heels, she soars down the path until a fallen tree branch stabs her foot.

She crashes to the ground, screaming.

Cradling her wounded foot, she pinches the end of the broken spear as it lodges itself deeper inside. Pulls on it. Cries out in agony.

Tamsen appears at the crest of the ridge, tiptoeing down the path. She slows as she recovers Nadia's shoes discarded in the center of the path.

"Where's my brother, you fucking bitch?" she shouts into the air.

Just then, Tamsen spies Nadia further up the path. She charges at her, screaming, and raising the blunt end of the axe high above her shoulders. Bringing it down, she slams the handle against Nadia's head.

NADIA HANGS UPSIDE DOWN, HUNTER'S NETTING SECURED AROUND her ankle tightening as it dangles from a tree branch.

Her eyelids snap open. Wide-eyed. Coughs as she labors with every painful breath.

Her palsied hands reach behind her head. Then, passes her hands in front of her eyes.

Fingers—wet with blood.

She winces, head throbbing.

Just then, a circle of light washes her blood-smeared face.

She squints, raising her arms to shield her eyes.

Tamsen approaches, aiming the flashlight on her.

"Please. Don't," Nadia begs, squirming as her body dangles there. "I was only doing what I was told."

Lightning flickers, Tamsen's hate-filled face blinking in the light. Her eyes—blazing with fury.

Thunder rumbles in the distance.

"Where is he?" Tamsen asks.

Nadia moans, her speared foot thrashing against the net. Tamsen brandishes the axe.

"WHERE THE FUCK IS HE?"

Nadia swats at her, pleading. Her final defense.

"He's—still in the game," Nadia says.

Tamsen's light searches Nadia's face. She watches as metal spikes sprout from Nadia's head, vein-thin wires circling the woman's throat until they form a black collar.

"You're not Nadia," she says.

Nadia's voice—frail and distorted. "He was supposed to set us free. And you ruined it, cunt."

Suddenly, Nadia's body snaps in half as if she were a rag doll.

Tamsen recoils at the sight. Nadia convulses—transforming.

A giant metal drum surfaces between her shoulders, bending her over until she resembles a hunchback.

Pistons and cranks burst through her clothing.

She rakes her head back, screaming. Reveals a valve fixed where her mouth used to be. Gears swirl, removing her skin.

Tamsen raises the axe, slamming the blade against Nadia's face. The screech of metal against metal.

She strikes her again, black sludge hosing her face.

Nadia's oil-slimed head rolls to the foot of the tree.

An engine uncoils from its hiding place, slithering out from the hollow iron rod of Nadia's severed vertebrae.

The creature scampers across the ground, rearing at Tamsen, before it dies.

Tamsen wipes the oil from her face, panting. "Fuck."

She soars up the embankment. Spots the framework of the Silo hidden behind the portico of trees at the forest's edge.

Sprinting down the causeway, she comes upon a deep trench.

Peering down, she finds a sheet of canvas blanketing the ground.

Tamsen crawls down the embankment. Skating to the edge of the canvas, she rips back the material and reveals –

A mass grave.

Naked bodies arranged in a large pile like firewood, snarling limbs twist around one another in a puzzle of human anatomy.

Tamsen covers her mouth, circling the pyramid of corpses. "Oh my God."

She sees a familiar face confined to the entanglement–a decapitated death mask framed between an elbow and a kneecap—Nadia.

Draped beside Nadia's body—Dani. Her face barely recognizable, crinkled and revealing bits of wires beneath her skin.

Another familiar face catches Tamsen's attention. She covers her mouth, realizing.

"Mr. Zimpago," she whispers.

Abbas Zimpago. The glassy, unblinking stare of a martyr. His throat—slit, the wound cemented brown with dried blood.

A naked older woman is sprawled over Zimpago's lifeless body. Dried blood as thick as wax, drools from the hole in her shoulder. Tamsen's eyes scrunch, trying to recognize the woman. She can't.

Tamsen skirts away from the mass grave, sidestepping tangled limbs. Scaling the trench, she climbs to safety.

Wiping the mud smeared against her clothing, she recovers the axe beside a rock.

"I'm coming, Pres," she says as she begins to make her way toward the Silo.

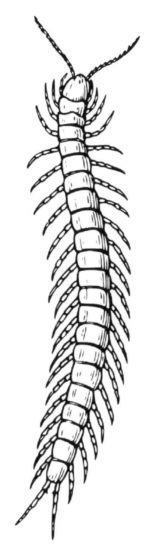

You've lost a lot of blood . . .

THE BONE KING: January 4th, 2019

There's something unnatural, something so deliciously grim, when you consider what we'll become in due time— when you consider how our fragile bodies will break down and rot, entropy and decay claiming us before we're nothing more than a mere human stain: a sculpture puzzle of bones, a liturgy of human anatomy that once was and will never be again.

I think of that often. I think of how unfair humans have it when compared to precious insects—little creatures without morality or burden of fear. Integrity is a foreign language to them. They don't speak in compassion or understanding. They know nothing of manipulation and degradation—things only human beings could invent to pit one against the other. Insects merely wish to survive like all other living things.

There's supposedly a type of cockroach that can live for an entire week without its head if it's been decapitated—a headless creature foraging, feeding, fucking, desperately trying to live and maintain its place in the food chain. I think of myself as that cockroach. Crawling toward oblivion without a head and franticly straining to survive no matter how terribly the world might want me to perish.

Of course, I scarcely expected myself to live past the age of twenty-five. I certainly could never imagine myself rotting inside a box for all of eternity—skin dripping away, maggots burrowing in hollow sockets, remnants as pale as moonlight left in my body's place. I'd rather push ingots into both of my eyes than feed earthworms in a hole in the ground.

If that's where I'm to end, then what's the point of any

of this? None of this has meaning. You and I have no worth, no real consequence if you look at it objectively.

Life has no meaning. If that's the case, why shouldn't I take it? Especially if they deserve to be killed for finding sexual satisfaction in something so ghastly. Bodies are not made of honeycomb. They're not made of wax. Ever since the invention of skin, the human body has been a vessel of mystery—a purposeless shadow of oneself, something to be revered for its complexity but also never understood.

And perhaps that's the point. Maybe we're not supposed to understand our purpose here.

But if that's the case, what's the point in carrying on like this? Carrying on like a puppet of some ancient deity with pubic hair as thick as fishermen's ropes.

There's no point to any of this.

They've started to refer to me as "The Bone King" because of my penchant for removing one of my victim's bones before I abandon the body. Would we do the same for a cockroach? Am I no better than an insect that scurries beneath a nearby desk when the lights come on? Tell me, I'm asking.

There are Queens in certain bug colonies. Just as there's royalty for humans—a privilege, a birthright to be born into. Humans and bugs aren't as far removed as one might imagine. And maybe that's intentional. Maybe they're a way for us to see ourselves outside of ourselves—a way to understand our cruelty, our sadistic behavior, our manipulation.

I'd rather be a cockroach without a head than continue carrying on like this.

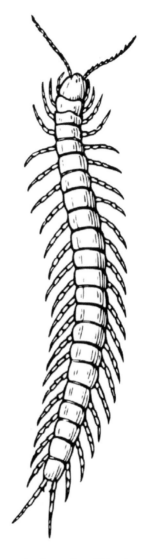

You've lost a lot of blood . . .

CHERNOBYL[1]

Skin like moth-eaten cloth, a mouth that frowns easily
and seems to know well the vertebrae of despair
Fingers crawling across every notch, every nook of bone
I might have once thought he was handsome
Might have once blushed in his presence
And taken to thoughts of the two of us—
Our sweat webbing together, our lips eager
To make confession of our most private thoughts
He doesn't keep me waiting there long,
Doesn't seem bothered when I ask if everything's alright
He's already pinning my body's most vile secrets
to the small board and gesturing to
The x-ray as if it belonged to someone long since dead—
a secret language lovingly buried in hemlock and ivy.
He circles the tumor in my brain with his index finger
and explains things will get worse before they get better
Even if they get better, that is.
He uses words like "malignant" and "stage four"
Then other words like "chemotherapy" and "terminal"
I think I can sense it when I close my eyes—
my mind's most shameful secret, a lewd thought armored
with
spikes and centipede feet to carry it toward oblivion
I feel the small pebble whirl inside the riverbed of my mind
Drowned by a gentle current, a voice that only speaks when
no one is listening.

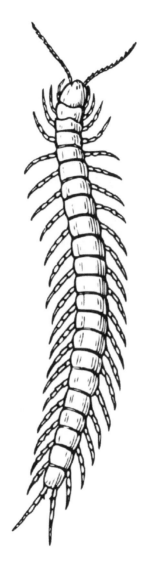

You've lost a lot of blood . . .

ALL THIS HAPPINESS MAKES ME SAD: February 1, 2019

[The following transcript was recorded on the afternoon of February 1st, 2019 with Martyr Black's cellphone. The recording was one of the several found among his possessions. The text written in italics was recorded over the original recording by Martyr Black.]

MARTYR: I could do it right now. Yes. It wouldn't take much at all. Just a flick of my wrist. Like when an artist invites paint to a canvas. Ambrose is my canvas—my grotesque creation in the making. There's something about him—something I can't quite explain that makes it difficult for me. Difficult to consider following through and hurting him. Of course, the thoughts are plenty. There's certainly no shortage of thoughts. But there's something that always stops me before I actually go through with it—before I take the hammer in my hands or before I grip the knife's handle to make good use of the blade.

AMBROSE: You know, not every living thing wants to live.

MARTYR: What made you think of that?

AMBROSE: Seemed appropriate.

MARTYR: Given?

AMBROSE: Given that we're cleaning up the poor boy's blood.

MARTYR: I once read somewhere that blood can be used as a substitute for eggs when baking.

AMBROSE: I suppose you'll expect me to order a *Frittata a la sangue* the next time we visit Italy.

MARTYR: Careful. You're dripping everywhere.

AMBROSE: Have you thought of that?

MARTYR: The carpet. Yes. You're making a mess.

AMBROSE: No. What I had said—not every living thing wants to live.

MARTYR: I suppose it's true. Haven't given it much thought.

AMBROSE: Why not?

MARTYR: He's always going on about the inanest things. Things most people wouldn't even consider. Then again, Ambrose isn't like most people. I suppose that's why I first fell in love with him—because I could tell he saw the world differently. If whimsy were a language, Ambrose would be fluent.

AMBROSE: Are you listening?

MARTYR: What did you say?

AMBROSE: There are some living things that want to die.

MARTYR: It's true for humans. Suicide is usually at an all-time high in the winter months.

AMBROSE: For animals, too. You've heard of animal suicide?

MARTYR: Hasn't been proven.

AMBROSE: The theory's been around for centuries. You've heard the story of the black dog in the *Illustrated London News*?

MARTYR: Can't say I have.

AMBROSE: It was first reported in 1845. The dog apparently threw itself into the river and remained perfectly still, presumably accepting its fate before rescuers arrived and snatched the dog from the water. But that didn't seem to stop the dog as only moments later it leapt back into the water and finally succeeded in its mission.

MARTYR: Careful. The carpet . . . Over here.

AMBROSE: There have been stories of cats hanging themselves from branches after their kittens perished or accounts of whales deliberately stranding themselves on beaches. For Christ's sake, even Aristotle wrote about a stallion that allegedly leapt to its fate on purpose.

MARTYR: And you're convinced that these animals were suicidal?

AMBROSE: You're not?

MARTYR: It seems to me that it's an all too human projection of a romanticized image of suicide that's been perpetuated by our culture.

AMBROSE: Take for example, honeybees. There are types of bees that will deliberately explode their own genitals. Just for an opportunity to pass along their genes.

MARTYR: Yes. Precisely. That's the point. To pass on their legacy. To provide for the next generation. Suicide is usually more inwardly focused. There's a considerable difference between being suicidal and being a kamikaze for the good of your species.

AMBROSE: One could easily argue that the Japanese pilots in World War II had a distinct death wish—that they chose to crash their planes into enemy ships and artillery because they wanted to die.

MARTYR: It was for the good of their people—to take out the enemy and to bring honor to their country.

AMBROSE: Honeybees will also voluntarily remove themselves from a hive if they suspect they've been infected with something that will compromise the integrity of the colony, effectively killing themselves as they knowingly perish without the support of the hive.

MARTYR: Yes. Once again, for the good of the community. Suicide is not a thoughtful act.

AMBROSE: What about that kind of parasitic worm that infects crickets and grasshoppers? It controls their minds and makes them leap into water where the worm can proliferate.

MARTYR: Not really an argument that supports your claim. It's the insect equivalent of being murdered.

AMBROSE: Yes. Why don't we hold bugs accountable?

MARTYR: Yes?

AMBROSE: A type of parasitic worm attaches to a host —a grasshopper—and compels the poor creature to kill itself so that the worm can multiply in its preferred setting. Why don't we hold the worm accountable for the grasshopper's demise?

MARTYR: Because the worm doesn't know any better. It just wants to survive. That's all it knows.

AMBROSE: That's what we're doing, too.

MARTYR: Yes, but one could argue that the young gentlemen we come in contact with—and eventually dispatch—are in no way impeding our fight for survival. Human beings kill for sport.

AMBROSE: Animals do too.

MARTYR: Yes.

AMBROSE: Zooplankton, damselfly naiads, predaceous mites, martens, weasels, honey badgers, jaguars, leopards, lions, spiders, brown bears, American black bears, polar bears, coyotes, lynxes, minks, raccoons, dogs....

MARTYR: Didn't realize I was talking to National Geographic.

AMBROSE: So why don't we hold them to our same standard?

MARTYR: Because—humans are supposed to know better.

AMBROSE: Do you know better?

MARTYR: *What's that supposed to mean? Is he having second thoughts about this? Is he trying to say something to me? Is this like the philosophical equivalent of comparing dick size? Ambrose knows why I kill these young men, why I've spent so much time and labored so diligently to make certain I'm never caught. He's helped me this far; he's cleaned their blood from his hair. If I'm guilty, then he is too. I can never let him forget that.*

MARTYR: Yes.

AMBROSE: Do you?

MARTYR: I'm not sure I understand what you're asking.

AMBROSE: Are you a coyote killing for sport or are you a parasitic worm that only wants to live?

MARTYR: I suppose I'd say I'm the worm. But then again, I'm not the grasshopper. The grasshopper might feel differently.

AMBROSE: I suppose our perception of animal suicide has afforded animals certain privileges they weren't privy to earlier.

MARTYR: Like?

AMBROSE: You can thank Charles Darwin for that— linking humans and animals. After years of tabloids reporting the tragic accounts of animals flinging themselves to their deaths, animal rights advocates would use these horrible stories to convince others that animals were psychologically complex and, therefore, deserved more compassionate treatment.

MARTYR: I suppose it is cruel to poke needles in the wings of baby birds or saw off the tusks of elephants.

AMBROSE: "All cruelty springs from weakness," according to Lucius Annaeus Seneca.

MARTYR: Is he saying that I'm weak? Is he implying that I'm a monster because of what I do, because of what I've dedicated my life to?

MARTYR: I think that saying implies that there's no direction, no purpose to the cruelty. Sometimes there is.

AMBROSE: I guess it depends on what we're talking about. Are we talking about the Japanese Unit 731 or are we discussing a little boy that's discovered what it feels like to tear the legs off a frog?

MARTYR: Unit 731?

AMBROSE: You know, the research and development unit of the Japanese army. To conduct experiments on humans to improve the efficiency of their military.

MARTYR: *Men Behind the Sun*[1]?

AMBROSE: I knew you'd seen it.

MARTYR: We watched it together, didn't we?

MARTYR: Did we watch it together? Suddenly, I can't remember. I only seem to be able to remember the scene where one of the soldiers has their arms and hands frozen solid, one of the officials cracking their extremities off and them screaming in agony—something quite irreversible. They looked like something monstrous, something out of a Hieronymus Bosch painting.

AMBROSE: It was a piece of exploitation trash.

MARTYR: How can you say that?

AMBROSE: You'd defend that film?

MARTYR: It was a moving portrait of one of Japan's darkest secrets—a dark stain on their history.

AMBROSE: *That film* is a dark stain on their history. Exploitative. The work of degenerates. The same people who praise that film are probably the same people that cream their pants over anything Darren Aronofsky directs.

MARTYR: You know full well *mother!* [2] was a cinematic masterpiece.

AMBROSE: Try "surrealist trash."

MARTYR: You think a film that layered, that textured is garbage?

AMBROSE: It's a two-hour masturbatory session. Vapid. No substance. Bland at best. Most critics weren't fooled by Aronofsky's prowess as a director, instead calling him out for a film that's so remorseless, so tasteless that it's an insult to the viewer.

MARTYR: Everybody's a critic.

AMBROSE: Isn't it unfortunate that nobody is credited for inventing that expression?

MARTYR: What?

AMBROSE: "Everybody's a critic." It was certainly invented. Someone had used it for the first time once and it's since been diluted in its original meaning so that now it's used to confess annoyance more than anything.

MARTYR: That's the best word to describe me and Ambrose —"diluted." That's the word that best describes what we've become. If relationships were physical things and not figurative constructs, then they would be parasites. Love between two people always changes who you are.

AMBROSE: How does it look?

MARTYR: As clean as a dentist's teeth.

AMBROSE: He looks peaceful. Lying there. Almost as if he were sleeping. As if he had asked us to do this to him.

MARTYR: It's what you had said—not every living thing wants to live.

AMBROSE: Do you think he wanted to live?

MARTYR: The way he pleaded with me, the way he begged. I suppose he did.

AMBROSE: But you wouldn't listen to him.

MARTYR: A worm doesn't listen to a grasshopper.

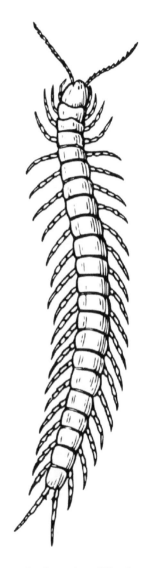

You've lost a lot of blood . . .

EUCHARIST

Gas mask covering a child's face,
and I had asked them where their
mother had gone, but they couldn't
speak because apparently kindness
to them was as scarce as hen's teeth.
I might have stayed, might have
pretended I wasn't afraid of the
morgue of little bodies under white sheets,
little ghosts waiting to be absolved by
men wearing surgical masks and
their breath as rusted as iron.
But I was distracted, beguiled by
a man's face without a nose—
a purse's zipper where his mouth once
was and now a slit where I can
pass coins through in exchange for
stories of horrible things he had done.
If I had looked closely enough,
I would have noticed he had two
rows of teeth—a secret kept there,
something obscene, something hideous.
If skin hadn't been invented yet,
I might have noticed how his lungs
were fixed where his brain was supposed
to be. Two satin pillows the color of puce
hanging there behind his ears and inflating
with his every inhale and exhale.
He smiles at me with a graveyard of rotted teeth
where his mouth should be—a voice
that tells me, "this body is not for you."

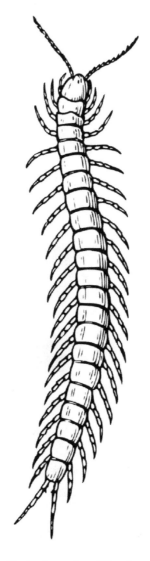

You've lost a lot of blood . . .

YOU'VE LOST A LOT OF BLOOD:

PART SIX

[The following text includes the final two chapters of a novella, You've Lost a Lot of Blood, *that Martyr Black had published by Carter Hill Press in October of 2018.]*

CHAPTER FIFTEEN

Tamsen lurches into the clearing of tall grass and bolts toward the massive structure.

Lifting the window-paneled doorway, she hesitates as the dark jungle of machinery stares back at her.

"Presley," she shouts into the labyrinth.

She grips the axe with intent, vanishing inside the building.

Darting down the narrow stairwell, Tamsen descends into the low-ceiling vault of concrete. She approaches the open steel door leading to the First Simulation Chamber.

The control panel flickers alive, bathing the wall with a holographic keyboard. Slams her finger against the button —Launch Sim.

Tamsen sprints inside the simulation chamber.

The door closes behind her, locking. Thud.

The Hive, a sparkling island like a spacecraft floating against the velvet curtain of the cosmos.

Tamsen scales the illuminated gangplank, the giant mechanism rotating on the exalted platform. She slides the doors open, climbing inside the vessel. She shoves the transparent helmet over her head. Channels of light spiral across the visor as the appliance connects to the USB.

She winces, a needle launching from inside the USB and stabbing the back of her neck.

"Fuck."

Tamsen wraps the belt around her waist, sliding her arms and legs into the restraints.

The Hive rotates, the platform lowering as the mechanism sinks beneath the chamber's floor.

Another thud. The whirring of a hydraulic pump lifting.

The Hive resurfaces from the sludge-filled vat.

The machine comes to a full stop as it settles on the platform. Tamsen waits. Eyes dart around, unsure. The pod door hisses, sliding open.

She lifts the helmet from her head, unfastening her belt and removing her arms and legs from the restraints.

Crawling out from the vessel, she scans the area surrounding the machine.

A labyrinth of machinery.

Columns of wire-laced devices stacked on top of one another rise until their vertical maze disappears from eyesight.

Boilers and generators neatly form endless rows, broad steam-swept corridors stretching to infinity.

Tamsen covers her mouth, realizing she's inside the game.

Swallows hard, eyes searching the massive pillars of machinery.

Notices pain-washed human faces buried inside the intricate structure of each mechanism.

A familiar face appears in the mosaic of machinery: The Old Woman from the convenience store.

"Take the child to Him," the Old Woman says. "The boy's the only one to set us free."

Tamsen winces in disgust, watching as wires slither out from the Old Woman's open mouth.

She covers her ears, the shriek of metal scraping against metal nearly knocking her over. The sound passes.

Tamsen creeps down the corridor. Peering down the passage, she searches for her brother.

"Presley!"

She glares at her reflection in the dark surface.

Tamsen wades into the channel, the oily sludge lapping at her waist. Lifting her arms above her shoulders, she meanders further. Notices the *You've Lost a Lot of Blood* symbol painted on the side of a half-sunken boiler.

She stiffens, tense.

The repeated thud of something large approaching.

"What the fuck–?"

Turning, her eyes cramp with dread. She sees it:

A giant wrought iron creature looming a hundred yards away.

Its face—the wrinkled mask of ABBAS ZIMPAGO.

The Zimpago-Engineer's massive body - suspended in the air by a complex framework of iron stilts and scaffolding it uses to steer down the canal like the oars of a gondola.

The Zimpago-Engineer unfurls his giant wings, honeycombed with rivets and piping.

He screeches as he approaches. The machines rumble at the deafening pulse of his echo. Tamsen ducks underneath a small ledge, hiding. Sludge laps against her from the creature's massive wake.

She watches the Engineer navigate down the flooded

corridor until the iron behemoth disappears down another channel.

Tamsen wades further down the pathway.

She slows as she reaches a grotto filled with transparent latex pods built on top of one another.

Various cranks and gears form columns along the walls as well. They rotate, humming, as if busy at work.

Each wire-gowned latex pod–swollen with the dark outline of a human body. The bodies—writhing in visible agony.

Tamsen searches the maze for her brother.

"Presley!"

A hydraulic arm jettisons from deep within the wall's scaffolding, clamping around Tamsen's throat and squeezing.

Tamsen screams, wires launching from the pods and coiling around her arms.

The machine lifts Tamsen from the sludge, cramming her body inside an empty pod and tightening the vessel shut.

In the pod, Tamsen squirms as oil sprinkles her.

A vent above her head vacuums the air from the pod, the latex gluing to her body until she can't move. Tamsen watches the silhouette of the hydraulic arm approach. The mechanical arm braces her mouth, inserting a surgical mouth prop and widening her jaws.

She gags, a wire snaking down her throat as the surrounding machines hum with labor. Pushing against her latex prison, she fishes inside her pocket. She pinches the snake earring, pressing the dagger-tip against her tightening coffin. A large tube filled with an engine lowers from the scaffolding outside the pod.

The arm guides the tube toward Tamsen's open mouth.

Tamsen saws faster.

The earring finally stabs through the material, the pod splitting in half. Tamsen spills out, her greased body crashing into the channel.

She swims away from the machine's reach, spitting the wires from her mouth and vomiting.

She notices the framework of the wall stirring in a frenzy—gears revolving, pistons firing.

Light glows within one of the pods, a shape forming. The silhouette of arms and legs sprouting from a dark center.

Tamsen wades further down the submerged passage, a severed wire scattering electrical sparks across the surface.

"Presley," she shouts.

She sees something floating in the center of the channel —the paper swan Presley had made. She grabs it, stuffing the soaked paper in her shirt pocket.

A deafening thud.

Tamsen retreats beneath a small shelf of machinery, her backside pinned against a pod. A shadow within the pod stirs. Tamsen jumps, startled. The restrained figure groans in agony. It's a familiar sound: Presley.

"Tam... Tam..."

She claws at the material, dragging her nails down the latex and splitting the sheet open. Presley's oil-soaked body shoots out of the pod, dropping into the canal. Splash.

Tamsen cradles her brother.

"Pres," she whispers. "Oh my God."

She yanks off the wires and cables glued to his face. Rips the small tube from his open mouth. Pales when she notices small metal spikes dotting his cheeks, the outline of wires curling beneath his skin.

She shakes his body, whimpering.

"Pres."

He grows limp in her arms.

Tamsen pats his lifeless body, touching his mouth. Moves his lips, as if a final plea to make him to speak.

Her voice—a pitiful whisper. "Please."

An engine explodes from Presley's mouth. Tamsen screams, hurling Presley's body away from her. The black centipede plunges into the canal, sinking beneath the surface.

Tamsen retrieves her brother's dead body before it floats away. She holds him close.

One of the pods above her splits open, releasing a giant black sac and tossing it into the canal.

The sac bobs on the surface for a moment. Then, sinks like a stone.

Another nearby pod opens, expelling a similar black sac and jettisoning it into the flooded passageway. The bag vanishes.

Tamsen swallows, watching as bubbles form in the channel.

An oil-slimed head surfaces. Hands wipe its sludge-smeared face clean, revealing—Tamsen's face.

A facsimile.

Tamsen covers her mouth in horror at the sight.

The Tamsen-Clone stares at her for a moment. Tilts its head, as if bewildered. Its eyes fill with fear.

Then, another head surfaces from the canal's dark mirror.

A facsimile of Presley.

The Presley-Clone looks around, frightened. His eyes lock on Tamsen. Trembles, panicked.

"Pres?" Tamsen says.

The Tamsen-Clone grabs the Presley-Clone by the arm, dragging him down the channel and away from Tamsen.

Tamsen lunges at them, hauling the remains of her lifeless brother across the canal's surface.

"Wait," she calls after them.

As she runs, she doesn't notice a dark shadow stir within one of the pods. A face presses against the translucent latex, revealing Nadia. Her mouth open in a silent scream.

The Tamsen-Clone scales the small ramp, hauling the Presley-Clone from the depths of the flooded passage.

They reach the Hive, climbing inside the vessel and sliding the door shut.

Tamsen dashes up the ramp, hastening toward the giant device. She flings open the doors. The clones are nowhere in sight. Flecks of sludge trickle down the vessel's empty seat.

Tamsen loads Presley's lifeless body into the Hive. Then, climbs inside. Drags the door shut and waits. The hydraulic system hums, the mechanism rising.

Tamsen pulls Presley close, watching as oil laps against the vessel's small window until it finally resurfaces.

Pulling Presley out of the vessel, she drags his body down the sludge-covered gangplank and through the Silo until she's outside. The Tamsen and Presley clones are nowhere to be found.

Kneeling at the building's entrance, Tamsen lifts Presley's lifeless body in her arms and carries him into the field of tall grass.

She meanders toward the forest as rain begins to sprinkle.

Passing by the carriage house, Tamsen notices her car is

now gone—puddles of black sludge pooling along the ground.

Eventually, she reaches the main house. Tamsen carries Presley across the driveway, climbing the house's front steps.

Ambling into the foyer, Tamsen spreads Presley's body out on the marble floor.

Her ears perk at the muffled sound of sobbing. Upstairs.

Grimacing, she recovers the dagger Nadia had abandoned beside the door. Then, creeps up the staircase until she reaches Zimpago's bedroom.

Tamsen appears in the open doorway, brandishing her weapon.

Peering inside, she finds Iris draped over the bed. The woman stirs, burying her face in Zimpago's stomach and sobbing.

Tamsen hesitates, Iris' deafening cries piercing through her.

Tiptoeing toward the bed, she senses the knife loosening in her hands. Grips it tighter, raising it with intent. Light flickers in her eyes, reflected in Zimpago's black goggles.

Before another moment of hesitation—Tamsen drives the knife into Iris' back.

Iris howls in agony, convulsing. Tamsen stabs her again. This time, in the shoulder. Iris lurches forward, weakening. Slides off her brother's body. She slumps onto the floor, hands twitching until they slow without movement.

Tamsen lunges at Zimpago's motionless body, driving

the knife into his stomach. Then, into his chest. He doesn't resist. Doesn't even move. She recoils, confused.

Tamsen snatches the black goggles from his face, revealing—Presley's eyes.

Gazing at her, unblinking. Vacant and glassy.

Tamsen covers her mouth.

Unraveling the bandages, she exposes Presley's face. A death mask. His skin—ashen. His lips—glued shut with dried oil.

Tamsen shrinks away, mouth open in disgust. "No."

Iris rolls over on the floor, shrugging off her black headpiece. Turns, revealing –

It's Tamsen's face.

Tamsen whitens at the sight. Shakes her head in disbelief. The Original-Tamsen stirs, blood creeping from under her.

"How could you—waste a second chance again?" the Original-Tamsen asks.

Tamsen searches the Original-Tamsen's face, trying to comprehend. "I—didn't... I never..."

"I—thought you'd change everything," the Original-Tamsen whispers. "You have to help him next time. He needs you."

Tamsen brandishes the dagger. "What the fuck are you?"

"You don't recognize the thing that created you–?... You were my second chance. My clean slate."

"You–?"

"Make sure they go into the game together next time," the Original-Tamsen says.

"Who?"

"They'll come back."

"How do you know?" Tamsen asks her.

"You did."

Tamsen shrinks, realizing. "I–?"

"Presley's the only one who can destroy Him," the Original-Tamsen says.

"Who–?"

"The Engineer."

Tamsen hardens, scared. "I'll burn the place to the ground."

"And ruin your only chance of being set free?"

"Free," Tamsen says, as if not understanding the word.

"Guide the boy," the Original-Tamsen says. "You need him. He'll set you free. Clean slate."

Light dims from the Original-Tamsen's eyes. Her head slumps to the side, mouth hanging open.

Tamsen approaches the mirror beside the bed. Studies her reflection. Her eyes widen when she sees it –

A wire slithers up her throat, beneath her skin. Her face heats red, the outline of a gear revolving beneath her cheek.

CHAPTER SIXTEEN

Tamsen removes the Original-Presley from his bed, arranging his lifeless body next to the Original-Tamsen on the floor.

She drags their bodies from the room.

As she kneels, the paper swan Presley had made falls from her shirt pocket and skates underneath the bed. She doesn't notice it.

Dragging their bodies into the forest, Tamsen shoves the Original-Tamsen and the Original-Presley over the edge of the trench.

Toppling down the embankment, their bodies land beside Dani and Nadia's headless corpse.

Revisiting the main house, Tamsen returns the recently cleaned tactical hammer axe to its glass case.

She returns the dagger to the fixture on the wall.

Then, she visits Zimpago's office. Tamsen crouches on the floor, setting the silver snake earring beside it.

She replaces the small figurine she had broken with another statuette.

Finally, the task she had been dreading:

Tamsen hurls her brother's lifeless body onto the bed in Zimpago's bedroom. Then, she begins swaddling him with linen bandages.

When she's finished dressing him, she slides Zimpago's black goggles over his eyes.

More machinery sprouting from beneath her skin, Tamsen arranges the Original-Tamsen's black headpiece over her head.

———

THE NEXT DAY, TAMSEN—HER FACE MASKED AND GOWNED IN expensive-looking black—waits outside the warehouse with a large blanket. Her eyes—trained on the building's massive doorway.

Two figures, drenched in oil, stagger out from the shadows: Dani and Nadia.

They amble out from the warehouse, into the light. They scan the area, panicked. See Tamsen.

Tamsen holds out the blanket for them. An offering. They hesitate, approaching. Take the blanket.

"Follow me," Tamsen says.

Tamsen leads Dani and Nadia away from the warehouse.

———

AFTER GUIDING THE NEW FACSIMILES OF DANI AND NADIA TO THE main house, Tamsen leads Nadia and Dani into the marble entryway.

She motions to the drawing room.

"Go wait in there," she says to Dani. "I'll bring you fresh clothes."

Dani obeys, withdrawing.

Nadia flinches as Tamsen turns to her.

"Come with me," Tamsen says, leading the puzzled woman deeper into the house.

NADIA, CLEANED AND DRESSED IN NEW CLOTHING, SITS BESIDE THE fireplace in the library. She's wrapped in a blanket.

Tamsen delivers her a cup of tea.

"Do you remember this place?" Tamsen asks her.

Nadia looks around, bewildered. "I think—I came here before. To meet with–"

"Ms. Zimpago."

"Yes," Nadia says.

Nadia squints, as if straining to see beyond Tamsen's mask. She realizes, blushing. "Oh. It's you. I'm sorry, Ms. Zimpago."

"Do you remember what you were doing in the warehouse?" Tamsen asks.

Nadia's cheeks heat red, embarrassed. Shakes her head again.

"Don't go back there unless I tell you to," Tamsen says.

Nadia merely nods.

"You'll stay in the East Wing," Tamsen says, heading for the library's door. "I'll show you to your room. Every door in the house instantly locks and can only be opened by using these scanners."

Nadia hastens after Tamsen.

Tamsen and Nadia stand in front of the window looking into Abbas' bedroom.

Presley, wrapped in bandages, lies without movement on the bed.

"You'll be expected to look after my brother as part of your daily tasks," Tamsen explains.

Nadia looks concerned. "Is he–?"

"Under no circumstances are you to enter that room," Tamsen says, her voice firming. "You'll report to me if anything changes."

"Changes–?"

"Do you understand?" Tamsen asks.

Nadia shrinks with caution. "Yes."

"We have two guests arriving soon," Tamsen explains. "You'll be expected to look after them and see to it they're comfortable."

Tamsen glides down the corridor, disappearing.

She doesn't notice how Nadia's eyes linger on the linen-wrapped figure in bed.

Tamsen peers out the attic window, down at the driveway.

She watches her car meander up the drive, slowing as it circles the grassy island in front of the house.

The Tamsen-Clone appears, climbing out of the car.

Tamsen watches the Presley-Clone surface from the vehicle, dressed in his sparkling gold lame suit.

She howls in agony, the outline of generator tenting beneath her clothing as the massive form splits her vertebrae in half.

Her shoulders inflate with gears, pistons pumping.

Limping toward the window, she looks down and watches as Nadia emerges from the house and greets them.

She presses her wire-threaded hands against the glass. Swallows hard, breath growling.

A wire shoots across her face. Beneath the skin. Circling the device, hooking its sharp tip into one of the ridges.

"Clean slate," she whispers, her breath filled with metal.

For a moment, she's sentimental—her humanity far from being completely bewitched. She imagines she's a small bird soaring above the Zimpago estate.

The steep-pitched roof. The narrow ledges filled with leering iron statues like guards.

Tamsen's car—parked and idling on the driveway. She watches as new versions of Tamsen and Presley approach Nadia with muted greetings.

As Tamsen imagines soaring higher, the surrounding forest comes into view as if it were an emerald curtain draped over a model.

There's something fake about the property as the view broadens further. The greenery looks artificial.

From a distance, the once monstrous house now resembles a miniature mock-up from a video game.

Tamsen flies higher, the forest's edge arriving in the view. Beyond the property, a vast emptiness sweeps in every direction.

The miniature replica—a small island of greenery surrounded by the widening maw of oblivion.

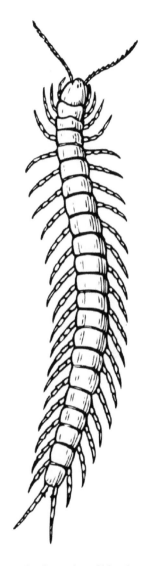

You've lost a lot of blood . . .

PARASITE: May 3rd, 2020

[The following transcript was recorded on the morning of May 3rd, 2020 with Martyr Black's cellphone. The recording was one of the several found among his possessions. The text written in italics was recorded over the original recording by Martyr Black.]

AMBROSE: You've lost a lot of blood, my love.

MARTYR: Why is he saying that to me? What have I done? What's happened to me? I feel like a starving Venus fly trap.

AMBROSE: We're going to stop the bleeding and take you to the hospital.

MARTYR: What happened?

AMBROSE: You don't remember?

MARTYR: Of course, I don't remember what happened. How could he even ask me that? It's as if time had become soup for me. A liquid to pass through. Something for my bones to soak while I melt away.

MARTYR: I—can't . . .

AMBROSE: You took the pen and stabbed yourself in the neck with it.

MARTYR: Please . . .

AMBROSE: Don't move. I'm trying to stop the bleeding.

MARTYR: Why did I—? Please . . . Help me . . .

AMBROSE: I saw what you were writing.

MARTYR: Yes.

AMBROSE: It's the same thing that boy in Chelsea had written . . .

MARTYR: The boy in Chelsea?

AMBROSE: Yes. You stole it from him, didn't you?

MARTYR: Of course, I stole it from him. I steal from everyone, everything. I don't have an original thought in my head.

Everything I have ever thought has been ladled into my brain and pushed around there like bits of broken sea glass.

MARTYR: What are you saying to me?

AMBROSE: You're a plagiarist.

MARTYR: Funny how we invent words to destroy a person's character.

AMBROSE: The words mean nothing. It's how they're used.

MARTYR: Yes.

AMBROSE: The way you chose to use them makes you a thief. You always have been. All those stories you made me read. All those poems you pretended belonged to you. They didn't, did they? They belonged to other minds, other hands that wrote them.

MARTYR: Yes.

AMBROSE: You stole everything from them. That's why you killed them.

MARTYR: Yes.

AMBROSE: I don't know anything about you, do I? They say that if you read what someone's written you can tell a lot about them—who they are as a person. I can't say the same for you. I know nothing of you. You've kept those parts hidden. Maybe once you could've shared your most private thoughts with me—your most shameful desires—but you pretended to be someone, something else.

MARTYR: Because I detest who I am.

AMBROSE: Is that why?

MARTYR: Don't you? Don't you hate who you are just a little? I'd like to meet the completely self-aware person who's enraptured with themselves, in love with their entire being. That person doesn't exist. And if they do, they won't be alive for long.

AMBROSE: Why did you steal from them?

MARTYR: Because I loathe the thoughts in my head. Because it seemed easy at the time.

AMBROSE: Because you didn't think you'd get caught?

MARTYR: No. I knew I would. I just thought you'd be dead by the time it happened. All those years being told I was a genius, that I would do such wondrous things in my life. Adults love to say those things to children. It hurts them more than they could ever know. Because when a child grows up to live averagely—to live a mediocre life—they think they've failed somehow. And perhaps they have. But it's really the adults that have failed them. It's the adults that have misguided them into thinking that they were special, that they were destined for such greatness that never came. So, I tried to invent my own greatness. Using others.

AMBROSE: I wanted to love what you wrote because I know that all writing is an extension of the creator—a message from them to share with the world. But I knew it wasn't yours. I couldn't love that part of you—the part that steals, that takes from others.

MARTYR: I don't think I've ever wanted anybody to truly know me, to let them love me.

AMBROSE: Why?

MARTYR: It felt like weakness. Letting them in, I mean. I didn't have anything original to offer to the conversation. I'm just a carbon copy of things that have been done before. There's nothing new that I can offer to the world.

AMBROSE: The bleeding's stopping.

MARTYR: I can't go to the hospital.

AMBROSE: Where would you have me take you?

MARTYR: Far away from here. There's nothing left for me here.

AMBROSE: There's nobody left here for you to plagiarize.

MARTYR: That's not it.

AMBROSE: Oh? Nobody left here for you to hurt.

MARTYR: I don't want to hurt anyone anymore.

AMBROSE: You don't expect me to believe that.

MARTYR: Come with me. I won't write anymore. No more killing. No more hurting people. That part is over.

AMBROSE: Where can we go? Who will take us?

MARTYR: We'll find a place.

AMBROSE: You make it sound like we're going to some far away, distant land.

MARTYR: Maybe we are. Maybe our brains are teeming with little parasites that are guiding us toward destruction. But I'd rather be there than here.

[This was the last audio recording located among Martyr Black's possessions.]

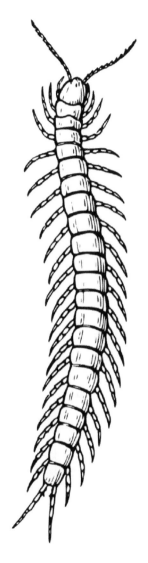

You've lost a lot of blood . . .

[A FINAL NOTE FROM THE EDITOR]

Although much of the text compiled in this edition has been lifted from various other authors, the editors of this book have been granted permission to reprint much of this material thanks to the compliance and gracefulness of the victims' families.

While Martyr Black's current whereabouts remains a mystery to this day, it is now assumed he was building a legacy of plagiarism with his writing as well as his crimes. The murders he organized of the various young men from which he had stolen countless pages of writing were displayed for authorities as if they were homages to various iconic European paintings.

This text was not compiled to titillate or excite the reader, but rather present a damaged mind on display and further explore the intricacies of Martyr Black's thought process while he successfully accomplished evading authorities and avoiding suspicion of plagiarism for several years before his and his partner's ultimate disappearance.

The editors of this text would like to thank the victims' families for being so agreeable and for allowing us access to information and documents otherwise kept hidden from the public eye. None of the writings presented in this manuscript were penned by Martyr Black. These writings were a crude patchwork—a Frankenstein's monster—of other people's thoughts and feelings.

The only accuracy to learning of Martyr Black—the person he once was—and his companion can be found in the transcripts of the recordings made between both he and his partner. It is somewhat surprising Martyr devoted so much time stealing ideas from others as he was such a decidedly opinionated person to begin with.

As chief editor of this edition, it is my sincerest hope that those directly affected by Martyr's destruction find closure. Some might question the need for publishing the work of a murderer, a plagiaristic parasite, etc. The answer for such an inquiry can be found in a quote once made by David Leavitt: "Sometimes brutality is the only antidote to sorrow."

Trent Pilcher
Cambridge, MA
August 2021

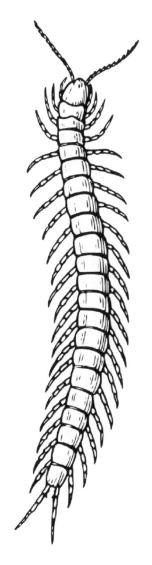

You've lost a lot of blood . . .

NOTES

RELICS FROM THE NIGHT WE BOTH PERISHED

1. *Chess* was a musical with a libretto penned by Sir Tim Rice and with music written by *Abba* front men Benny Andersson and Bjorn Ulvaeus. The musical began life initially as a concept album released in 1984. The album spawned countless hit singles including, "One Night in Bangkok" and "I Know Him So Well." After the success of the concept album, a theatrical production was mounted on the London stage in 1986. Due to the success of the original London production, *Chess* transferred to Broadway in 1988 but the production was ultimately panned by critics.

I SEARCH FOR YOU UNTIL MY LUNGS SPROUT METAL

1. Many have speculated that this particular poem, "I Search for You Until my Lungs Sprout Metal," was written by Martyr Black during a period of time when he was contemplating writing a book of poetry detailing the disastrous nuclear fallout at Chernobyl in 1986. This particular poem (along with many of the others printed in this edition) was published in a collection by Carter Hill Press in the spring of 2018.

STORIES YOU CAN'T TELL AT PARTIES

1. John Carpenter's 1982 film *The Thing* is an adaptation of the classic science-fiction horror novella *Who Goes There?* written by John W. Campbell. The film starred Kurt Russell and featured special effects orchestrated by Rob Bottin.
2. Robert Wise's 1963 film *The Haunting* is an adaptation of Shirley Jackson's classic novel *The Haunting of Hill House*. The film is widely considered one of the finest haunted house films in the genre.

TOMB_GIRL_GIF: MARCH 10TH, 2019

1. Originally titled *The Forgotten, Don't Look in the Basement* was an independent horror film directed by S.F. Brownrigg and written by screenwriter Tim Pope.
2. Henry Fuseli's painting *The Nightmare* was the first of its kind in the romanticism period. For those unfamiliar with the perverted spectacle, the painting details a young woman thrown across a divan with a stout, hairy incubus perched on her chest and staring menacingly at the viewer. In the background, a black mare enters the scene through lush, red curtains.
3. Another equally celebrated painting from the 19th century. *La Grande Odalisque* depicts a young woman, supposedly a member of a harem, reclining and gazing at the viewer.

BODIES MADE OF HONEYCOMB: DECEMBER 7TH, 2018

1. Sir John Everett Millais' painting of Ophelia was completed in 1851 and 1852, and depicts the character from Shakespeare's play, *Hamlet*, singing as she drowns in a reed-strewn river.

CHERNOBYL

1. This particular poem, "Chernobyl," was written not long after Martyr had murdered his first victim. As you will discover, Martyr often wrote poetry from the point of view of his victim. In this poem, he assumes the role of an individual with a cancer diagnosis and being groomed by another for sexual service.

ALL THIS HAPPINESS MAKES ME SAD: FEBRUARY 1, 2019

1. *Men Behind the Sun* is a 1988 Hong Kong exploitation horror film directed by T.F. Mou. The film has become notorious among cinephiles for its graphic depictions of the cruel medical experiments endured by prisoners warehoused in Unit 731.
2. *mother!* is a 2017 psychological horror film written and directed by Darren Aronofsky. The film stars Jennifer Lawrence and Javier

Bardem and recreates Biblical stories through a traditional horror lens.

ABOUT THE AUTHOR

Eric LaRocca (he/they) is the Bram Stoker Award-nominated author of several works of horror and dark fiction including the viral sensation *Things Have Gotten Worse Since We Last Spoke*. He is an Active Member of the Horror Writers Association and currently resides in Boston, MA with his partner.

For more information, please follow @hystericteeth on Twitter/Instagram or visit ericlarocca.com.